HOME ALONE

Still sniffling, but feeling infinitely better, I hurry into the keeping room and open the closet beside the fireplace.

I reach up and feel around the ceiling for the hidden lever.

"Eeeeuuuuhh!" My hand has just brushed something soft and filmy—cobwebs. "There better not be any spiders up there," I mutter to myself.

Then I stop. Did I just hear something behind me?

Several things happen simultaneously.

I belatedly remember that I forgot to lock the kitchen door . . .

I start to turn around . . .

My fingers find the lever and the secret door springs forward . . .

I realize I'm not alone . . .

And I discover, with sheer and numbing horror, exactly what happened to the missing meat cleaver.

"Please," I say in a tiny, trembling voice. "Please don't hurt me with that."

"How dare thee?" Elspeth asks, her voice low with venom, blocking the doorway of the closet. "He is mine. I have loved him since we were children. *How dare thee?*"

"What are you talking about?"

"I saw thee locked in an embrace with Zachariah."

"With Zachariah? I was only comforting him, Elspeth." I stare, mesmerized, at the gleaming silver blade that's only inches from my face. My mind is racing. She's insane.

And she's dangerous.

Books by Wendy Corsi Staub

HALLOWEEN PARTY

WITCH HUNT

Published by Pinnacle Books

WITCH HUNT

Wendy Corsi Staub

PINNACLE BOOKS
KENSINGTON PUBLISHING CORP.

www.pinnaclebooks.com

PINNACLE BOOKS are published by

Kensington Publishing Corp.
850 Third Avenue
New York, NY 10022

Pinnacle and the P logo Reg. U.S. Pat. & TM Off.

First Printing: March, 1995
First Pinnacle Printing: September, 2000

Printed in the United States of America
10 9 8 7 6 5 4 3 2

*For four special people
who love me unconditionally—
my grandparents:
Pasquale and Della Corsi & Sam and Sara Ricotta*

And for Mark, again . . .

With special thanks to Jon "The Big Man" Gifford
and "Uncle" Bill Pijuan, for their cheerful and
constructive assistance with research
in Salem, Massachusetts

ONE

6/14/63

Dear Brian:

I know we just said goodbye, but I had to write and tell you how much I miss you! I don't know how I'm going to get through a whole summer away from you when I'm already going cuckoo and it's only been a few hours! Right now, we're stuck in this Friday night traffic jam outside Boston. My parents are making us listen to Glen Miller on the radio, and it's not even coming in that well. Peter and Paul keep fighting over some stupid comic book they both want to read—as if they aren't loaded down with hundreds of them. And all I'm doing is staring out the window at the dumb honking traffic and thinking about how much I miss you. This summer is going to be so—

"Hey, cut it out!" I holler at my brothers, who are battling over the comic book on the seat next to me. One of the little monsters has just nudged my arm and made my pen draw a jagged line off the edge of the stationery and onto my bare leg. "Look what you made me do! Mom!"

I spit on my finger and rub at the ink mark. I think about how Josie Kurtzenbaum told me that if ink gets on your skin it can seep through your pores and into your blood and poison you.

My mother looks into the backseat and sighs. "Boys, how about if we play the license plate game again?"

"That's no fun. They're all Massachusetts," Paul says, scowling and tugging the comic book again. Peter is gripping the other side and scowling right back at him.

"That's not true. Look, I see a Rhode Island one right there." My mother points cheerfully. "And there's Maine . . ."

No one is interested in the game, which she made us play all the way out of New York City and into Connecticut, when my father finally overthrew her as leader of the car and demanded silence so he could concentrate on the traffic.

I don't know why they had to be in such a rush to leave the city. They should have known traffic would be bad on the Friday night before the first summer weekend since school got out. I don't see why we couldn't have waited until tomorrow morning—or even Monday.

Or never.

I think about Brian Burleigh, the boy who finally asked me to go steady on my birthday just last month. I've liked him ever since last summer, when he broke up with Linda Kramer, but he didn't seem interested in me until my best friend Josie Kurtzenbaum told his best friend Louie Colettini that I liked Brian. And even though it took him almost the whole school year to ask me out, it was worth the wait. I bet he'll give me his class ring to wear around my neck when he gets it in September. I can't wait—I keep picturing Linda Kramer's face when she sees it.

Anyway, everything was just about perfect until my father's Great-Uncle William—whom I'd never even heard of before—died a few weeks ago and left some big old house in Massachusetts to my grandparents. But Grandma and

Grandpa Harmon, who moved to Miami last year, didn't care about the house and told my father he could have it if he wanted it. If you ask me, it was their way of helping us out without offering a handout, which my father would refuse. But they know how hard it is for him to feed a family of five in New York City on a teacher's salary.

My parents drove up to Seacliffe—that's where the house is—to take a look at it a few weeks ago. And when they came back, they announced that we were going to spend the summer there and they were going to fix it up so they could sell it.

They acted like the news would thrill my brothers and me.

"Just think," my mother said, "we'll be out of the hot city for the whole summer."

"I don't *want* to be out of the hot city. I *love* the hot city!" I hollered, even though I'd spent the past few summers complaining about how most of my friends got to go to camp up in the Catskills and it wasn't fair that I couldn't. I knew that was kind of selfish of me because I know darn well my parents can't afford to send me, but I couldn't help it.

But this year, even though most of my friends are still leaving for camp, I would have had Brian, who spends the summers working at his father's clothing store on Eighth Avenue. And Josie, whose parents can't afford camp either.

I pleaded with my parents to let me stay in New York with Josie's family or with my mother's sister, my Aunt Donna. But my mother pointed out that there are already seven kids in the Kurtzenbaum family and they're spilling out of their three-bedroom apartment.

And ever since Aunt Donna left Uncle Nicholas and started working as a cocktail waitress at some supper club downtown, we haven't seen much of her. I guess my parents think she's a little crazy, and letting me stay with her was out of the question.

So here I am, in the backseat of the Chevy on a stupid highway leading to stupid Seacliffe, Massachusetts.

"Who are you writing to, Abbey?" my mother asks, turning around again to peer into the backseat. "Siobhan?"

Siobhan is my pen pal. She lives in England, in this small city called Liverpool. She's the one who told me about this swell new singing group from her town. They're called the Beatles, and you should see how great-looking they are! The moment I saw their picture in the newspaper clipping Siobhan sent, I was in love. For my birthday, she even sent me one of their records and a beautiful silver Beatles pendant on a chain that I've been wearing around my neck day and night. Ringo is my favorite. I kiss his carved little silver face every night before I go to sleep.

"Right, I'm writing to Siobhan," I lie to my mother. The last thing I need is for her to get started in on Brian and how I'm only sixteen and too young to be going steady.

"That's nice," she says, smiling and turning back to look at the road just in time to shriek at my father, "turn here! This is it! Frank, slow down! That was it . . . back there!"

And he curses and slams on the brakes and we all go flying, and as he grumbles and backs the Chevy along the shoulder toward the road we just missed, the road leading toward Seacliffe, Massachusetts, I groan and wish I were back in good old hot, sweaty New York City.

"You're kidding, right?" I ask my parents. "This isn't it."

"This is it!" my mother repeats happily, and my father pulls the Chevy into the driveway alongside the big old house—the ugliest, scariest house I've ever seen.

"This place looks haunted!" Paul echoes the words that are running through my mind. "Neat-o."

Peter, the more timid of the twins, just stares at the house, his blue eyes round and worried.

"It's not haunted," my father says, turning off the car and stretching. "It just looks a little scary because it's nighttime. When you see it tomorrow morning in the sunshine, you'll love it."

The three of us in the backseat glance at each other doubtfully.

Then I look back out the window. When my parents described the place to us, I had pictured a quaint old house with a gingerbread porch, shutters and window boxes, and maybe cupolas and a widow's walk.

Uh-uh.

This gloomy-looking place is two stories high and shaped like a big ugly box. There's no porch, no window boxes, and the shutters at the paned windows are mostly missing slats and some of them are hanging crookedly. The walls are made of horizontal narrow wooden slats that look weather-beaten and are covered in some peeling, drab paint, the color of which is impossible to tell in the dark.

"Just think . . . the house is almost three hundred years old!" my mother chirps.

"Great," I mutter. "Just great. Does it have indoor plumbing?"

"Of course it does, Abbey," my father tells me, opening his car door. Instantly, a chilly, damp breeze blows in. It smells like fish and salt and algae. I guess we're right next to the ocean. I wrinkle my nose.

"It may have a bathroom but it doesn't have a hi-fi," I grimly remind my father. Was I ever upset when he told me that! I brought my Beatles record anyway—I didn't want to leave it back in New York, where someone might break into our apartment and steal it.

My father ignores me and slams his door behind him.

"Come on," my mother says, getting out of the car, too. "Let's unload the trunk."

Sighing, I open the door and step out into the pitch-black night. Paul does, too.

We don't notice that Peter has stayed put until we're standing by the open trunk and my father is handing out bags.

"Where's Pete?" he asks, picking up my brother's little blue duffel bag.

"He's being a big sissy," Paul informs us. "Says he's not coming out."

My mother and I walk back around and look inside the car. We see him huddled in the backseat with his arms wrapped around his knees and his eyes all big and spooked.

"Petey, what's the matter?" my mother asks, opening the door.

"Nothin'."

"Come on out, honey," she coaxes, showing him his duffel bag. "We need you to carry this inside."

"I'm not going in there," he says stubbornly.

"I don't blame him," I put in.

My mother shoots me a look and then says to Peter, "Why not, honey?"

"It's haunted."

"Oh, Petey, it is not. You're going to love this house."

Both my brother and I look dubiously at the wooden monstrosity looming above us in the dark sky.

"I don't think so," I say helpfully. "I think we'd better not stay here. It doesn't look . . . safe. Let's go back to New York."

"Abbey, stop that," my mother says as my father comes

up behind her suddenly and says, "What's going on here?" which makes us all jump out of our skins.

See? I guess even my mother is a little jittery about this creepy old house.

"Petey is afraid of the house," my mother says, stroking my brother's stubbly blond summer crew cut.

"What? Don't be silly. There's nothing to be afraid of. Come on, Pete, be a man."

"Yeah, be a man," Paul echoes. "Who's afraid of a few ghosts?"

"Ghosts?" Peter squeezes his eyes shut.

"Paul, you know there's no such thing as ghosts," my mother says firmly. "Now, Petey, if you'll come inside, I'll let you have first choice about which bedroom will be yours."

My brothers, who sleep in bunk beds in our apartment back in the city, had been all excited when they found out they'd each get their own room in the summer house.

Now Peter's eyes snap open and he protests, "I don't want my own room! I want to sleep with Paul."

"Uh-uh," Paul says firmly. "I get my own room."

"Then I'm not going in," Peter says again, setting his jaw.

My parents look at each other. Then my father says, "Pete, you're ten years old, going on eleven. You don't want anyone to call you a sissy, do you?"

Personally, I think that's mean of my dad to say.

Poor Peter just shakes his head miserably.

"Well then, come on inside."

"And if you'd like to sleep with Paul just for tonight, you can," my mother says.

"No, he can't," Paul says immediately. "I get my own room. You said."

"He can sleep with me," I offer, patting my little brother's shoulder.

Peter looks up gratefully. "I can?"

"Sure."

"Thank you, Abbey," my mother says as my father shakes his head, takes out his key ring, and walks toward the house, followed by Paul, who's also shaking his head.

"It's no problem," I tell her.

I'm not willing to admit that I'll be glad to have Peter around.

There's something strange and foreboding about this big old house. I can't put my finger on it, but I get the feeling that something isn't quite right here.

My heart is beating really fast and I can't shake this weird sense of apprehension as I walk toward the front door.

I hate old stuff.

Particularly this house.

If it looked bad on the outside, it's even worse on the inside. The first thing that hits me when I step into the front hall is a musty, stale scent that my mother poetically describes as "aged wood and antiques and memories and history . . . and isn't it wonderful?"

Personally, I think it stinks.

And the place is ugly, too.

Almost every room has this faded old-fashioned wallpaper that's torn away or curling in some spots. There are exposed beams everywhere you look, and the ceilings are so low that even I feel as though I have to keep ducking, and I'm only five foot six.

There aren't any overhead lights, and the lamps are ancient and throw off a yellowish glow that doesn't reach into the shadowy corners of the rooms. And there are so many of them—rooms, I mean—that I can't keep track and I keep getting lost.

Not to mention the fact that the rooms all seem cramped and are much smaller than the ones in our apartment back on East Eighty-third Street. There's one exception: a long room that runs along one whole half of the first floor, which my mother proudly refers to as the "keeping room." I guess it's sort of a seventeenth-century version of a rec room. It has a gigantic fireplace I can stand in, and lots of built-in cupboards and shelves. There are more windows in this room, too, and they run almost from the floor to the ceiling, so it doesn't seem as depressing as the others.

To get to the kitchen, you have to go through a narrow passage off the keeping room. There's another enormous fireplace in there, and my mother told me people actually used to cook in it. There's a little brick oven built into the inside wall, too.

"Hey, where are the bedrooms?" I hear Paul asking my father from the front hall, where they're coming in with more bags.

"Upstairs. Here, hold on to this for a second," my father replies.

Paul groans audibly. "Hey, this is heavy! Come on, Dad. I want to pick my room before Abbey gets the best one."

"In a minute, Paul. You have to be my helper right now."

Naturally, I make a beeline back to the front of the house and up the narrow staircase. It's so steep it's practically a ladder, and the steps are uneven. Nice. Real nice.

At the top, I see a dark, close corridor lined with doors and lit only by a naked bulb. It looks pretty creepy.

Gathering my courage, I start opening doors and peeking into the dark rooms. They're all small and crowded with ugly old furniture, and everything is musty-smelling and silent. I'm feeling more and more jumpy, as though a ghost is going to pop out at me any second now.

I'm just closing the last door when I hear Paul's footsteps pounding up the stairs, followed by my mother's. I hear her saying, "Be careful, honey, these stairs are treacherous."

Instantly I make my decision. I'll take one of the larger rooms at the back corner of the house. It's only about ten by ten and there's no closet, but it's better than the rest of the rooms.

The bed is a narrow, creaky iron contraption that my mother, predictably, refers to as "quaint." But the mattress is so lumpy—and so are all the others—that my father comes upstairs, takes one look, and agrees to buy new mattresses and boxsprings first thing tomorrow.

My mother, the eternal optimist, points out that I have "a pastoral view" from my windows, but all I can see are a bunch of trees shrouded in fog.

Everyone else goes downstairs to have some Pepsi in the kitchen. I spend a few minutes opening drawers in the tall old dresser between the windows. They're all empty and lined with thirty-year-old newspapers that have headlines about the Great Depression.

Yuck.

I can't put my clothes in there. Everything I own will stink. I'll probably start to smell like a big must-ball myself.

My room is such a disappointment that I don't explore it for very long.

All right, maybe the real reason I don't want to be there alone is that I'm a little spooked. There's something strange about this house, and I don't like it one bit. I don't know how I'm ever going to sleep in this room every night if I can't even stay for five minutes. Thank goodness Peter will be with me tonight, even if it is going to be a tight fit on the narrow bed. Maybe I can talk him into sharing a room with me for the whole summer.

I hurry back downstairs, telling myself to stop being so silly. It's just an old house. And maybe my father was wrong and there really is a hi-fi. If I could just hear "Love Me Do," I'd feel a lot better.

But there's only an old radio set in the keeping room that's almost as tall as I am, kind of like the one my grandparents threw away when they moved out of their apartment in the Bronx. At least there's a television set—chalk one up for Great-Great-Uncle William—even if it is at least ten years old with a tiny round screen.

All in all, the whole place is depressing. I keep thinking of our up-to-date apartment back home with its Danish modern olive-green and brown living room furniture, the brand-new Frigidaire and twenty-three-inch television set my father just bought at Macy's, and, most importantly, the hi-fi.

But even worse than the outdated furniture and appliances is the strange, creepy feeling I can't seem to shake. This old house just isn't normal.

I stand alone in the keeping room, just looking around and half-listening to the voices of my parents and brothers in the kitchen, and half to the wind outside, and in the distance, the crashing ocean.

And as I stand here, the back of my neck prickles like crazy.

I know it seems ridiculous, but I'm really starting to get scared.

I can't seem to shake the feeling that we never should have come to Seacliffe. It's not just that I miss the city, or Brian and Josie, or the hi-fi . . . it's something more than that. Something much more serious.

I'm certain—and I don't know why, but I am—that something bad is going to happen in this house.

TWO

I'm dreaming that I'm lying on my side, clinging to the edge of a cliff over the ocean. Someone is trying to push me off, and I can't hang on any longer.

"Help!" I scream as I start falling . . .

And land, with a hard thump, on the hard wood floor.

I blink and look up to see Peter rubbing his eyes with his fists and staring at me.

"What are you doing down there, Abbey?" he asks as my father bursts through the door, followed by my mother.

"What's going on?" my father asks. "Abbey, are you all right?"

I'm still pretty dazed. Then slowly it comes back to me. I'm on the floor in my new room in the Seacliffe house.

"I must have fallen out of bed," I tell my parents, sitting up and rubbing my shoulder. "Ow."

My mother looks concerned. "Honey, did you hurt yourself?"

"No." The last thing I need is for her to hover over me, all worried.

"I *told* you guys that bed was too narrow for two people," my father says grumpily. "Tonight, Pete, you sleep in your own room."

Peter and I exchange a glance. He looks terrified, and I don't blame him. The two of us were awake for most of the night, unable to sleep. The house kept making weird creaking noises. And besides, it was so quiet outside—nothing except the sound of far-off waves and an occasional breeze.

In the city, my room faces the street, and I love to lie awake and listen to cars and voices and footsteps—you know, *normal* sounds.

"What time is it?" I wince as I get up and sit on the edge of the bed.

My parents shrug. We all look around for a clock, but there isn't one. Then I remember and check my watch on the table beside the bed. The hands are silently sitting at three o'clock. I guess I forgot to wind it.

The room is really bright, though. Sunlight is beaming in through the window.

"I guess we should be getting up now anyway," my mother says, yawning and stretching. "Come on, Petey, let's go find some clothes for you to wear."

Obligingly, my brother climbs out of bed and follows her. My father goes into the bathroom across the hall.

I go over to the dresser, bend over one of the drawers I left open to air out, and sniff.

"Yuck," I mutter, wrinkling my nose. Still musty.

Yawning, I open my suitcase and start making stacks of clothes on my bed, even though I don't know where I'm going to put them. But I feel as though I'm moving in slow motion. I feel exhausted. Maybe I'll sleep better tonight, without having to share my bed.

On the other hand, I'll probably sleep worse without Petey around. The thought of being alone in the dark in this house is terrifying . . . but I know that's ridiculous. It's just a house.

Still, even in the morning light, the place has a creepy feel. Just thinking about it makes me feel jittery, even though

I can hear my father running water right across the hall and my mother and Petey talking in the next room.

Stop being such a baby! I scold myself.

A few minutes later, I hear Paul, in his room down the hall, protesting as my mother tries to wake him up. She keeps telling him it's getting late.

Then he says, "It is not! Look at my watch. It's not even six o'clock yet!"

My mother starts to protest, then stops.

Suspicious, I go over to the door and stick my head out into the hall. "Mom?" I ask as she tiptoes out of Paul's room and closes the door behind her. "What time is it?"

Reluctantly, she says, "It's five-thirty-five."

"What?"

We both look at the sunlight streaming through the window at the end of the hall. My mother shrugs. "I guess it gets light a lot earlier here. After all, we're a few hours east of New York. Besides, it's almost the summer solstice, June twenty-first—the longest day of the year."

I just groan and go back to bed.

I can't believe how much I hate it here.

The second time I wake up, I go straight to the window and look out. The sun is almost overhead—it must be late enough to get up.

I can hear a lawn mower rattling across the grass next door. Curious, I watch to see who's pushing it. I have to wait a few minutes until he gets beyond the hedge that separates our yard from theirs. It's a boy. I can't tell how old he is or what he looks like from here. *He's probably just a kid,* I think cynically.

But he *is* pretty tall. He's wearing Bermuda shorts and a

baseball cap, and his shoulders look broad beneath his pale yellow shirt.

Just when I think maybe this is a good sign, I remember that I now am a girl who has a boyfriend. And I plan to be true to Brian no matter what.

So it shouldn't matter how old the boy next door is. It shouldn't matter if he's handsome or not. Even if he looks like Ringo, I will not pay any attention to him, I tell myself firmly.

Of course, if Ringo himself happened to show up, I can't promise I wouldn't forget all about Brian in a second. According to a British magazine clipping Siobhan sent me, all the Beatles have an adorable cockney accent. I saw *My Fair Lady* on Broadway before it closed last year, and Eliza Doolittle had a cockney accent. I'll bet it sounds even better coming from Ringo. I love accents.

I drop the curtain back over the window, blocking out the lawn-mowing stranger.

Out in the hallway, at the top of the stairs, I call, "Mom? Dad?"

There's no answer. The house is silent.

"Peter?" I call hopefully. "Paul?"

They wouldn't dare leave me all alone in this place . . . would they? The thought of it is so scary that I spring into action. I dash into the bathroom and wash and brush my teeth in the stained porcelain sink before hurrying back to my room to get dressed.

I decide against wearing my new olive-and-brown plaid Jamaica shorts and matching sleeveless brown blouse. I spent a month's worth of baby-sitting money on this outfit at Korvette's before I knew I wouldn't be in the city for the summer. These are the newest colors of the season, and I was imagining myself wearing the outfit for a movie date or maybe to Palisades Park with Brian.

Instead, I throw on an old pair of dungarees and a white T-shirt. Then I jerk a brush through my shoulder-length hair, carelessly tucking it behind my ears.

Normally, I would set the ends on orange juice cans so that they'd flip up, and I'd take more time to tease the top and sweep my bangs across my forehead.

But right now, I just want to get downstairs.

And besides, who cares how I look? Why should I bother with my hair? Who's going to see me here in dinky old Seacliffe, Massachusetts?

I slip my feet into my white Keds and practically fly down the stairs.

The house is quiet. A note on the counter in the kitchen announces that my parents and brothers have taken a walk into town.

I can't believe they didn't wake me up. Weren't they the least bit worried about leaving me all alone in a strange place?

Back in the city, up until last year, my mother still had our neighbor, Mrs. Gramucci, come over whenever she and my father went out to a movie or dinner. My brothers and I always hated that.

Don't get me wrong—Mrs. Gramucci is nice enough. But she smells like mothballs, and she hates television—she's afraid of the "dangerous rays" it gives off.

My mother always claimed Mrs. Gramucci wasn't baby-sitting, just "keeping us company." But finally, when I started baby-sitting for the people downstairs last fall, my father convinced my mother that we could do without Mrs. Gramucci's company.

But I sure wouldn't mind if she showed up in Seacliffe right now, mothballs and all, to baby-sit me.

I look around the old kitchen. The ceiling in here is a little higher than in the rest of the house. I vaguely remember my father saying something last night about how the kitchen was added on much more recently. Of course, that doesn't mean it's up-to-date. I'm beginning to sense that "recent" in Seacliffe might mean anything after the Civil War.

Apparently, my mother has put away the groceries we brought with us from New York. I look through the cupboards until I find a box of Special K, and pour a heap of it into a chipped bowl. Then I cross my fingers and open the icebox. Luckily, there's a fresh bottle of milk. My father must have gone out to buy it this morning.

I notice the words COLONIAL DAIRY on the side of the glass bottle as I remove the round paper cap. Does everything in this stupid town revolve around the past? Sighing, I pour some milk over my cereal and look around for a place to eat. I could sit at that wobbly-looking wooden table in the corner, I suppose . . .

But do I really want to be alone inside this creepy old house? It's so big, and the only sound is the old grandfather clock ticking in the next room.

No.

It's much too creepy.

I pick up my bowl and a spoon and slip out the back door. Out here, in the sunshine, I feel a little better. I sit gingerly on the rickety wooden steps and survey the yard. It's big and grassy and stretches way back to some woods. There seems to be a narrow path cut between the trees, and I remember that my mother said you could walk to the ocean from our backyard. I guess that's the way you go.

I notice that the sound of lawn-mowing is no longer coming from beyond the hedge, and wonder what the boy is up to now.

Not that I care.

"Hi," a voice says, and I jump so high I spill Special K and milk all over my legs.

I look up to see a girl standing in front of me with a dismayed expression on her face. "Look what I made you do! I'm so sorry."

"I . . . it's okay," I say through gritted teeth.

"Want me to help you clean up?"

"No thanks." Carrying my cereal bowl, with milk dripping down my bare legs, I start walking back inside. The girl is right behind me.

I turn around and give her the eye.

She just says cheerfully, "You must be Abigail."

I wonder how she knew that. "It's Abbey."

"Abbey. And I'm Katie," she goes, as if that somehow explains why she's here. When I just keep looking at her, she adds, "Kennedy."

"Kennedy?"

"It's my last name."

"Any relation to JFK?" I ask. After all, Seacliffe *is* near Boston, which is JFK's hometown.

She looks pleased at my attention. "My father says we're distant cousins."

"Oh." Usually I'm terrible with names, but Kennedy is pretty easy to remember.

"I saw Jackie once," she puts in quickly, lest my interest should fade.

"Where?"

"In a hotel lobby in Boston a few years ago. She was pregnant with John-John."

"That's nice. Well, I have to go wash this milk off my legs," I say, going up another step.

"I'll help you," Katie offers, right on my heels.

What can I do? Tell her she can't come inside with me?

Actually, I'm kind of glad to have the company. Anything is better than being alone in this house. Even hanging around with this overly friendly, polite girl who kind of reminds me of a female Eddie Haskell from *Leave It to Beaver.*

I notice that she's wearing a crisply ironed, full-skirted pink-and-white gingham-checked sundress and her long blond hair is caught up in a high ponytail tied with a pink bow. No one in New York dresses this . . . daintily.

I also notice that she's carrying a wicker basket covered with a blue-and-white checked cloth. I consider saying, "Who are you supposed to be, Dorothy from the *Wizard of Oz?*"

Josie would crack up at that.

This girl probably wouldn't get it.

She sees me looking at the basket and says, "Oh, I almost forgot. This is for you." She puts the basket into my hands.

"For me?"

"For your family. They're fresh cinnamon rolls. My mother baked them this morning."

"Oh, thanks," I murmur, because I don't know what else to say. I can't imagine why her mother would be giving away cinnamon rolls. I put the basket on the counter.

At the kitchen sink, I clean up while Katie chatters about how she lives next door and she was so excited when her mother told her a girl her age would be living in the old Crane house for the summer.

"Crane house?" I echo, drying myself off with a dish towel.

"That's what everyone in Seacliffe calls this place. The

family that used to live here in the sixteen hundreds was named Crane, and they—"

"Hey, did you ever hear of the Beatles?" I cut in, to shut her up. I'm definitely not interested in ancient history.

"Beatles?" She wrinkles her bobbed, freckled nose. "Ugh. I hate bugs."

"They're not bugs, they're boys."

Her face lights up. "They are?"

I guess she likes boys. "Yeah. They're a band from Liverpool, England, and they're great. I heard that most people like Paul, but Ringo is my favorite. I have one of their records."

"How did you get it?"

"My pen pal sent it to me. She lives over there. Want to hear it?"

"Sure," Katie says, flipping her ponytail.

"Okay."

She looks at me expectantly.

I shift my weight. "Uh, do you have a hi-fi at your house?"

"Sure. Why? Don't you have one?"

"No. This place doesn't have any modern conveniences." I shake my head and rinse out my cereal bowl in the sink. I wasn't hungry anyway.

"But it's such a historic house—wait till I tell you some of the stories about it!"

"Oh, boy," I respond, but my sarcasm is lost on her.

"This place is full of great old things, isn't it?" Katie is saying glowingly. "I love antiques."

"I *hate* antiques. And history."

She looks unfazed. She seems to be the bouncy, resilient type.

How annoying.

I think wistfully of strong-willed, opinionated Josie, who never backs down and is always ready for a good argument.

"Well then," Katie says, shrugging, "I guess you won't be interested in the Puritan Days festival."

"I guess not." I pause. "What's that?"

She flashes me a sunny smile. "It's an annual week-long celebration in town to commemorate the first settlers. It starts today, and it's a lot of fun. Everyone wears old-fashioned outfits, just like they wore in the sixteen hundreds. And there are concerts and pageants and craft booths . . . you'll love it."

I just look at her dubiously. "I don't think so."

"Oh, come on, Abbey, it's really fun. Maybe later we can walk down to the town commons. That's where everything is set up. And since we're probably about the same size, you can borrow one of my costumes."

"I don't think so," I say again.

Katie just smiles. "Come on. Let's go over to my house and play your record. My mom is making brownies."

Maybe I am hungry after all.

And even if Katie isn't Josie, I guess it wouldn't be a bad idea to make friends with her. At least I'll get to listen to "Love Me Do."

"And you can meet my brother, Riley," Katie says. "He just finished mowing the lawn, but I think he's still around. He has to go to work in a little while. He's a lifeguard at the beach."

Did she say lifeguard?

"He's eighteen," she adds.

Hmm.

"And I'll show you my doll collection, too. I have—Hey, Abbey, where are you going?"

"I'll be back in a second," I call over my shoulder. "I just want to run upstairs and change my clothes."

The inside of Katie's house is as dainty and fussy as she is. There are lots of flowered fabrics and little tables and doilies everywhere. And Mrs. Kennedy looks like an older version of Katie, only her hair is pulled back into a bun instead of a ponytail. She, too, is wearing a crisply ironed pink dress, along with an embroidered, starched apron.

Their kitchen smells wonderful—like cinnamon and chocolate and coffee.

"Have a seat at the table, Abigail," Mrs. Kennedy says, "and Kathleen will put some brownies on a plate for you girls."

I almost say, *who?* Then I figure out that Kathleen is Katie. I think Kathleen suits her better. I've always thought Katie was a tomboy name, and this girl is no tomboy, that's for sure.

"I met your parents when they came up to look at the house in May," Mrs. Kennedy says, pouring herself a cup of coffee from the percolator on the stove.

"Did you?" I say, for lack of anything better.

"Yes. They're lovely people."

I don't know what to say to that, either, so I just nod and smile politely. Katie shows up with a plate of brownies and sets them on the table just as the most handsome boy I've ever seen—aside from Ringo, of course, and Brian—walks into the room, saying, "Hey, Ma, can I borrow the car?"

"This is our Riley," Mrs. Kennedy says, smiling up at him. He must be at least six-foot-two. I can't tell what color his hair is—he's still wearing that baseball cap. I notice that it's a stupid Red Sox cap. I hate the Red Sox. He's changed into maroon swimming trunks and has on a white shirt that says *Lifeguard*. And he's very tan.

"Hey, who are you?" he asks, suddenly noticing my presence.

"Uh, I live next door," I reply, a little taken aback.

"Oh, are you related to those two identical little kids I saw out in the yard this morning? I thought I was seeing double."

"They must have been my brothers. Peter and Paul," I tell him.

"Oh, yeah? So who are you? Mary?" He whistles a few bars of "Puff, the Magic Dragon," then cracks up at his joke.

"Gee, that's a new one," I say, deadpan.

"Riley, stop teasing," his mother says. "Her name is Abigail. Abigail Harmon."

"Abigail. Sorry. So how do you like living in the old Crane house?" he asks, looking at me. He has beautiful sea-green eyes and long black lashes.

"In the Crane . . . uh, fine," I say stupidly. I wipe my suddenly sweaty palms on my new olive-and-brown shorts.

"Seen any ghosts yet?" He flashes a white-toothed grin.

"Ghosts?"

"Sure. It's haunted, you know." He and Katie are both nodding solemnly.

My jaw drops. I knew it.

"Riley, stop that," Mrs. Kennedy scolds.

"Ma, everybody knows—"

"Riley! Don't you listen to him, Abigail," Mrs. Kennedy says. "Katie, why don't you pour your guest a glass of milk?"

"I'll have a cup of coffee," I say hastily, "if you don't mind."

All right, maybe I've never even tasted coffee before. Maybe I am trying to impress Riley. So what?

The three of them look at each other.

"Of course," Mrs. Kennedy says, moving over to the stove.

"You drink coffee?" Katie asks incredulously.

"No, not coffee, Katie," Riley says before I can answer. "She drinks *co-awfee*." Then he flashes me that dazzling grin again.

I raise an eyebrow at him.

"What's the matter? Didn't anyone ever tell you you have an accent, Miss New *Yo-awk?*"

He's teasing me, and I'm thrilled that he's not a male version of Katie—nice and polite, but kind of boring. There's definitely something devilish about her brother.

"*I* have the accent?" I shoot right back at him. "You're the one with the accent, Mr. 'Can I borrow your *cah.*'"

He looks a little surprised at my spunk, then grins good-naturedly. "All right, Abigail. We're even."

"Abbey," I say.

"Abbey," he repeats as his mother puts the cup of coffee down in front of me.

"Cream or sugar?" she asks.

"No, thanks. I take it black."

There's a long pause.

"So, Ma, can I borrow your *cah?*" Riley asks again.

"As long as you just drive it to work and right home again."

"Well, I wanted to stop at the park on my way."

Naturally, coming from him, it's *pahk*.

Did I mention that I really love boys with accents? Riley's Boston one sounds a lot like JFK's.

"You're going to the park? Can we catch a ride with you?" Katie asks excitedly.

Riley shrugs. "Why not?"

Katie turns to me. "We can go walk around there for a

while. The park will be all set up for the festival. It'll be fun. You'll get to see all the costumes."

Oh, goody gumdrops, I think.

But on the other hand, it would be kind of fun to hang around with her brother for a while. He's the most interesting thing about Seacliffe so far. Of course, I don't *like* him, like him. I would never betray Brian. But still . . .

Riley grabs a brownie and pops it, whole, into his mouth. "Come on, if you're coming," he says, jangling a set of keys and heading toward the door.

I stand up. I'm really glad I changed into this new outfit.

"Do you want to bring a brownie along to eat on the way, Abbey?" Katie asks.

"All right." I pick one up and take a little nibble. It's delicious.

"What about your coffee, Abigail?" Mrs. Kennedy asks. "Don't you want to drink it first?"

I reach for the cup and take a tiny sip. "Oh . . . um, that's all right. I don't want to keep anyone waiting," I say, following Riley and Katie to the door.

What a relief.

I hate coffee.

THREE

If I thought things were looking up for a moment there, I was dead wrong.

The day takes a downhill plunge when Riley stops the car in front of a big old house on a shady street leading into town. The minute he toots the horn, a pretty girl with a bobbing blond ponytail comes bouncing off the porch. She's wearing a crisp pale yellow sundress and there's a matching bow in her hair.

She looks suspiciously like Katie. I wonder if all the girls in Seacliffe do.

"Hi there, Riley!" she calls, waving gaily as she comes toward the car, her ponytail swaying behind her head. "Hello, Katie."

Katie is hopping into the backseat, where I'm already sitting. "Hi, Trudy," she says. "This is my new friend, Abbey. She's living in the Crane house for the summer."

Trudy and I greet each other with a basic "Hi." Hers is considerably more cheery than mine.

Riley slings his arm across the back of the seat, against her shoulders, as he pulls the car back out onto the street. She giggles and snuggles into him like it's January and she's freezing or something.

I decide to write a long letter to Brian as soon as I get home.

The town of Seacliffe seems to consist of tree-lined streets lined with old white houses. Nearly all of them have porches and shutters, and there are American flags hanging everywhere you look. I guess it's a patriotic place.

Right smack in the middle of the town is a park. All four sides of it are lined with shops, and there's also a white steepled church and a redbrick town hall. *And* a movie theater, which excites me until I see what's playing. Alfred Hitchcock's *The Birds*. I saw it ages ago in New York, with Josie.

"Hey, neat-o," says Katie when she catches sight of the marquee as Riley slows down to find a parking space. *"The Birds* is finally here. I've been dying to see that. Want to go with me tonight?" she asks me.

"I already saw it," I tell her.

"Wow, you did? Was it gory?"

"Very." I proceed to discuss a particularly bloody scene in graphic detail. I talk loudly.

Up front, Trudy and Riley seem to be in another world. The car radio is blasting this song I used to love last year, "Johnny Angel," which I'm really sick of. In fact, I'm starting to hate it. Especially now that Trudy is singing every word, interrupting herself only to tell Riley how much she loves the song.

By the time I finish telling Katie about the movie, she looks a little disturbed and says maybe she won't go see it after all. Then she bounces right back with a buoyant, "Hey, did you see *Hud* with Paul Newman? Isn't he the dreamiest?"

The dreamiest? Eeeeuuuhh!

"He's all right," I say, even though, next to Ringo and Brian, I secretly love Paul Newman. "And I saw that movie ages ago, too. Have you seen *Cleopatra?*" I ask, even though I know darn well that she hasn't. It just opened in New York this week.

"The new movie with Elizabeth Taylor and Richard Burton?" she asks.

I have to fight an impulse to sarcastically say "no." It's only the biggest movie ever made, and the whole world has been talking about how expensive it was to film and how Burton and Taylor had an affair on the set.

I just nod at Katie.

"No, it hasn't come to Seacliffe yet," she says.

What a surprise.

"Have you seen it?" she asks me.

"Well . . . no," I admit. "And I suppose it won't start playing here until Christmas," I mutter under my breath.

Just then Trudy goes, "There's a spot, Riley!"

Riley maneuvers the Chevy into a diagonal parking spot near the town hall. The four of us get out.

I see that the park is set up with carnival-type booths, and it's jammed with people. Most of them are wearing old-fashioned, pilgrim-style clothes. If you ask me, they're all crazy. It must be eighty degrees in the bright Saturday sunshine, and here they are, bundled up in heavy dark colors and long sleeves.

Trudy's ponytail sways furiously as she bobs her head around excitedly. "Oh, I love Puritan Days," she announces, practically hugging herself with joy.

"So do I," Katie agrees. "Come on, Abbey. Let's go walk around."

"To-awk to you later," Riley says, catching my eye.

I just wave. "Nice meeting you, Riley. You too, Judy."

She giggles. "It's Trudy."

"Oops, sorry. I'm terrible with names." Which is the truth.

Then I turn and catch up to Katie, who's eagerly heading for the park.

"Is that his girlfriend?" I ask her.

"Whose girlfriend?" she asks blankly, looking around.

"Riley's." I toss it off casually, as though I don't care either way—because of course, I remind myself, I don't.

"Who? Trudy?" Katie asks.

"Who else?"

"Oh. Kind of," she says. "But Riley likes to play the field ever since he dumped his old girlfriend, Sherry, last summer. *I* don't believe in playing the field, though."

"You have a boyfriend?"

"Well, no," she admits. "But if I did, I'd be faithful. Do you have a boyfriend?"

"Yes," I say firmly. "And I'm faithful, too. Even though he's in the city and I'm here."

"What city?"

Boy, is she ever dense. "New York," I say impatiently.

"Oh, right." Katie nods, then glances around with an eager expression. Her face lights up. "Hey, do you want to go get a hot dog?"

"Might as well," I say with a shrug. That brownie only made me hungrier.

We get in line at the hot dog booth.

This pretty girl with her auburn hair in a flip hairdo comes by and stops when she spots Katie. "Katie Kennedy, I haven't seen you in ages!"

"Hi, Jeannie," Katie says, flashing her sunny smile.

"How have you been?"

"Oh, fine. This is my friend Abbey Harmon from New York City. Abbey, Jeannie Gladhart."

Katie sounds cheerful, and I notice she's trying to impress Jeannie by the way she says, "New York City." But if you ask me, that smile of hers isn't quite as bright as usual.

I greet this Jeannie person with a casual, but not too friendly, "Hi, nice to meet you."

"Nice to meet you," Jeannie returns briefly, giving me a once-over, then turning back to Katie. "Well, gotta go. I'm working at the balloon booth over there. Hey, tell Riley I said hi, and to stop by, okay? I'll be here all week."

"Sure," Katie says. As soon as she turns back to me, I remember something I need to ask her.

"Hey, Katie, what was that Riley said earlier about the house being haunted?"

I half expect her to say, "What house?"

But she doesn't. She just nods, her eyes getting all wide and solemn. "Well, I wasn't going to tell you, but you would have found out sooner or later."

"Found out what?"

"That the Crane place is haunted. Everyone in town knows it."

"Oh, great." I try to act indifferent, but my heart is beating pretty fast.

"Katie!" Two girls are calling her from across the grass, and she turns around.

"Oh, hi, Mary Beth . . . hi, Susie."

"Where's that brother of yours been hiding?" one of the girls, a pretty brunette in a headband, asks.

"Oh, around."

"Well, tell him hi for us," calls the other girl, a chubby blonde.

"Sure." Katie nods and waves, then turns back to me again.

"You know a lot of people," I tell her.

"Small town," is all she says. Then, "Anyway, as I was saying, no one is really surprised the place is haunted. You know who used to live there, don't you?"

"How would I know that?"

"Didn't you ever hear about Felicity Crane? It's a really famous story."

"Maybe in Seacliffe. Not in the rest of the world."

"No, it was in my history textbook last year," Katie says. "In the unit about the Salem witch hunts. You've heard of those, haven't you?"

"Of course." In fact, my mother brought them up just last night. We passed through Salem on the way to Seacliffe.

"Well, in 1692, which is the same year the Salem stuff took place, this young girl from Seacliffe was also tried and executed for witchcraft. She was only about our age. And she lived in your house."

"She was *executed?*"

"They hung her right over there, from a tree," Katie says, pointing across the park.

"Which tree?"

"It's not around anymore, Silly Goose!"

I'm thinking, *Silly Goose?* as she goes on, "That was almost three hundred years ago. But do you see that stone marker? There's a plaque on the front that tells the whole story."

I look where she's pointing and see a big gray rock.

"Want to go read about it?"

I swiftly shake my head and say, "No, thanks. That's all right. So you're telling me that Felicity's ghost haunts our house?"

"Sure, she probably does, too."

"Too? You mean there's more than one ghost?"

"Probably," Katie says again, twirling the end of her ponytail around her finger. "The most famous ghost is Jemima, though. She was one of the Cranes' slaves. She was from some island in the south seas, and people say she was a witch, too. One day, she vanished. People say that Felicity's father,

Josiah Crane, found Jemima doing witch things and killed her."

" 'Doing witch things'?" I repeat dubiously. "Like what?"

Katie shrugs. "Casting spells or whatever. Anyway, people say her ghost has been seen in your house."

" 'People'? Who are these 'people' you keep talking about?" I'm trying to make light of this whole thing so that I won't be scared out of my wits.

"Oh, I don't know. Just everyone," she says vaguely.

"How do they know it was Jemima's ghost?"

Katie shrugs again. "They just do."

Honestly! This whole business is ridiculous. "There's no such thing as ghosts," I say firmly, as much to Katie as to myself.

"If you say so." She's wearing this smug little smile. "You'll find out, sooner or later."

And despite my nonchalant, "Oh, sure," a chill slides down my spine.

It's Saturday evening, and I'm once again alone in the house.

After supper, my parents took Peter and Paul back to the park for some fife and drum concert that's part of this whole Puritan festival thing.

The four of them are really excited about living here—even Peter. It's been like a magical transformation. One minute, the twins are moaning about missing their friends and the Yankee games and the neighborhood street fair in July, and the next time you turn around, they're thrilled about this place.

Traitors.

They've kept chattering all afternoon about what a beautiful town Seacliffe is, and how much there is to do here, and on and on. They've even signed up for some day camp program that starts Monday morning. And they're all excited about going to some Red Sox game at Fenway Park in Boston with my father in a few weeks. They used to loathe the Red Sox.

See? I told you they were traitors.

And my parents, who have spent the afternoon unpacking and going around the house with tape measures and notebooks, planning their remodeling, are just ecstatic about Seacliffe, too.

They kept trying to talk up this concert tonight, trying to get me to go along to the park. But I refused to be swayed.

I didn't bother telling anyone that my idea of fun isn't exactly going to a fife and drum concert.

Or that I've had enough of this crazy town.

The more I saw of Seacliffe this afternoon as Katie showed me around, the more convinced I became that everyone here is obsessed with the past. All the stores seem to be called Ye Olde this or that, and there are little signs and markers everywhere that tell you when things were built, and by whom.

Katie was really proud when she showed me the plaque by her own front door that says, "Built in 1712 by Capt. Henry Waddington." And it turns out that our own house has one, too. It says, "Built in 1685 by Josiah Crane."

By midafternoon, I'd had enough of history being crammed down my throat, and enough of Katie, too. After we'd walked back from town, she wanted me to come inside and play my Beatles record, but even that didn't sound inviting. All I wanted to do was go home and be by myself.

She asked me if I wanted to come back to the park with her tonight. She was going to be wearing a costume, and I could borrow one too. The thought of wearing some three-hundred-year-old dress in public is about as appealing as going out stark naked would be. I made a face at Katie, who

seemed really disappointed, but I didn't care. She's perky.
She'll bounce back.

You should have seen how thrilled my mother was when
I told her where I'd been. She kept saying what nice people
the Kennedys are, and how delicious the cinnamon rolls
were, and so on and so on. By the time she quit talking, I
was even more sick of Katie, and her whole family, too.

Including Riley, who, incidentally, brought Trudy home
from the beach with him. I heard her giggle come floating
up to my window, and I looked out and saw them together.

So I basically spent the rest of the day on my bed, writing
a nice long letter to Brian, telling him how much I miss him
and how much I hate it here. I started a similar letter to Josie,
and came back up to my room after supper to finish it.

But now that everyone has left for the concert, I can't help
wishing I'd gone with them. I know, I know—fife and drum?

But frankly, anything might be better than being here
alone. I'll admit it. I'm a little scared. I can't stop thinking
about what Katie said—about how this house is supposed to
be haunted.

I take a bath in the old-fashioned tub and wash my hair,
and the whole time I'm in there, I'm jittery. I had wanted to
take a long, relaxing soak like I do back at home, but who
can relax here? I can't shake the feeling that something's
going to happen—and not something nice or pleasant.

After I'm all dried off and my hair is combed out, I sit on
my bed writing to Josie. I jump at every little sound the
house makes. And old houses make a lot of noise, did you
know that? They creak and groan and make what my mother
assured me are "settling" sounds. Don't ask me what that
means. She couldn't even explain it when I asked her.

At 7:30, I go downstairs to the keeping room to watch the
Jackie Gleason Show, which will be a welcome distraction.

But when I turn on the stupid old television, the picture is all grainy and I can't seem to get a vertical hold on it. And there seems to be something wrong with the sound, too.

After five frustrating minutes, I give up and turn off the set. The episode was a repeat, but I really wanted to see it anyway. Don't ask me why, but I would have felt a little safer . . . as if no ghost would dare haunt me when I'm watching Jackie Gleason.

It's getting dark out already, so I go around turning on every light in the house.

Back in New York in the middle of June, it's light until nine o'clock. But I guess since the sun comes up earlier here, it goes down earlier, too. I wish I'd thought of that when I let my family take off without me. I'm not particularly anxious to be alone here when it's dark outside.

For lack of anything better to do, I go back upstairs and flop down on my bed. Then I take out the new book Josie gave me as a going-away present. It's actually been out since last year, and I've heard a lot about it. It's called *Sex and the Single Girl,* by Helen Gurley Brown, and my mother would kill me if she knew I was reading something so trashy. I can't believe Josie had the nerve to march up to the register at Doubleday's and pay for it, but nothing ever seems to faze her.

I'm only a few pages into the book when I suddenly hear a loud sound from downstairs.

I bolt upright and listen.

There it is again.

A bumping, thumping noise.

And it's coming from the keeping room, right below my bedroom.

It's just the house "settling," I tell myself, as trepidation courses through my body.

I sit absolutely still, holding my breath and listening intently.

And within a few seconds, I'm positive that it isn't the house settling at all.

The sound is coming closer, up the stairs, and I'd recognize it anywhere.

It's footsteps.

FOUR

Oh my God, oh my GodohmyGodohmy—

Suddenly, I get a grip on myself. I can't just sit here panicking.

Someone is in the house!

What do I do?

Protect yourself.

Good. That's good. I have to protect myself.

Frantically, I look around the room. An object propped in the corner jumps out at me. It's my big, heavy, could-be-a-deadly-weapon black umbrella.

Carefully, I get off the bed. I expect the ancient bedsprings to let out a loud squeak, but they don't.

Fighting back terror and the urge to just bolt out of this place and run for my life, I tiptoe three giant steps across the room and grab the umbrella. It seems flimsier than I remembered. How am I supposed to fight off an intruder with this?

Especially if it's a ghost?

Don't be stupid, I instantly deride myself. *It's not a ghost. There's no such thing as ghosts.*

It's probably nothing at all. You're probably imagining the sounds.

Standing utterly still just inside the doorway of my room, clutching my umbrella, I listen intently.

No.

Those are definitely real sounds. They're definitely foot-steps. And they're definitely about to reach the top of the stairs.

I squeeze my eyes shut tightly and try to think rationally.

If I scream, would anyone hear me?

The walls in our New York apartment are so thin that Mrs. Gramucci next door hollers "God bless you" if one of us sneezes.

But this house is built like a fortress. And even if I did scream, and someone could actually hear me, there's no one nearby to hear me—except maybe Trudy and Riley. And do I really want the two of them rushing to my rescue? Especially if the intruder isn't someone who's trying to kill me?

But who else would it be?

Maybe it's my parents. Or Peter. Or Paul.

Relief courses through me. That has to be it. Someone came to their senses and left that stupid fife and drum concert.

Except . . . if it's someone in my family, why are they creeping up the stairs so hesitantly?

It must be Paul.

That's it. He's always sneaking up on people, trying to scare them.

But if it isn't . . .

I can't stand it. I can't just stay here in this room like a trapped, umbrella-wielding animal.

I have to take action.

I inhale a deep breath, open my eyes, and lean forward, poking my head out into the hall and turning it toward the stairway . . .

. . . just as someone appears at the top of it.

It's not Paul, or Peter, or my parents.

I'm so paralyzed by what I see that I can't move, can't make a sound, can only stare.

It's a man—or boy. Or someone in between.

And he's dressed all in black.

But not the kind of black clothes cat burglars wear.

The kind of black clothes people wore three hundred years ago.

Oh my God—it's a ghost!

That's all I can think as I stare at the person who's just putting his foot—clad in a pointy shoe with a big buckle—onto the floor of the hallway.

And as he steps up, I hear myself make a gasping sound. Startled, he looks around, then catches sight of me.

For an endless split second, we gape at each other.

Then I find my voice. "What are you doing here?"

I had intended a forceful shout, but it comes out in a whispery croak. For emphasis, I raise the umbrella over my head in what I hope is an ominous gesture.

He's just staring at me, as if he's confused.

And I'm slowly realizing that he doesn't *seem* like a ghost.

He looks solid and real.

And definitely not very threatening.

I take a step toward him.

That does it.

He bolts.

For a moment, I'm paralyzed.

Then I impulsively take off after him, flying down the steep, narrow staircase as fast as I can, and running through the house, following his pounding footsteps on the wooden floors. I'm still so unfamiliar with the layout of this place that I keep tripping over furniture and nearly slamming into walls.

By the time I reach the back door, he's escaped. I see him

running off across the dark backyard toward the little thicket of trees near the water.

I'm about to go after him when I suddenly think, *What am I, insane?*

I can't go chasing an intruder through those dark woods. How do I know he won't hurt me?

Then I think, *What, by shooting me with a musket?*

And then I think that I'm crazy to be joking—even with myself—at a time like this.

I mean, this is serious.

Someone broke into our house.

I lean weakly against the frame of the back door and concentrate.

I try to remember what the intruder looked like, exactly, so that I can identify him for the police later.

He was tall—not as tall as Riley Kennedy, but maybe almost six-feet.

And he had on a black coat and some sort of knickers. And a ruffly white blouse that had a giant white collar sticking out over the jacket. Kind of like a Peter Pan collar with points. Oh yeah—and his shoe had a big buckle on it, and he was wearing thick stockings, like knee socks or something. And a big, broad-brimmed, dark hat.

He'd basically looked like most of the men I saw in the park today, at the Puritan Days festival.

Except for his hair.

Even though he was wearing a hat, I could see his hair. Lots of it. It was dark brown and kind of wavy and shaggy.

Who do I know who wears his hair that way?

My father doesn't count. He's going bald.

But I think about my brothers, who both have crew cuts.

And Brian, who doesn't have a crew cut, but whose hair is pretty stubbly anyway.

And Riley, who was wearing a hat, but whose hair is also so short that I couldn't tell what color it is.

But Ringo . . .

And the rest of the Beatles . . .

They all have long hair that's kind of shaggy!

The intruder's hair was kind of like that, only longer.

And *more* shaggy.

Hmm.

I ponder this for a few more moments, and come to the conclusion that the intruder is probably British, like the Beatles.

Amazing.

I should consider becoming a detective when I grow up.

But even if the intruder is British—which would explain the hair—who is he?

And what did he want?

The most obvious answer is that he's a burglar who wanted to rob us.

And the more I think about that, the more it makes sense. Anyone who knows anything about Seacliffe would be aware that most people are out at that concert in the park tonight. That means that most houses are empty—the perfect opportunity for an enterprising burglar.

Even that weird pilgrim getup he was wearing makes sense. He was trying to blend in with everyone else in this nutty town. It was his Puritan Days costume.

That has to be it.

It has to, because there's no other explanation . . .

Except that the intruder was a ghost.

And I simply refuse to believe that.

There's no such thing as ghosts.

Besides, everyone knows this house is haunted by

women—Jemima the Slave Woman and Felicity the Teenage Witch.

I cling confidently to that knowledge, as if it somehow guarantees that the intruder who just fled wasn't a ghost—on the off chance that there really *are* such things as ghosts.

And I stare out into the dark yard, wondering what he's doing now. Is he hiding behind that clump of trees? Or is he already far away from here, in a getaway car?

Somehow, that doesn't seem likely.

I examine the back door, expecting to see marks where he broke the lock. But the lock is fine.

How did he get in?

After locking the back door, I roam from room to room, searching for a knocked-out screen or some sign of how he broke in. But I can't find anything. And I really, *really* want to.

Because that would prove that the intruder was a burglar—a *British* burglar, I remind myself—and not a ghost after all.

But the more I investigate, and the more I think about what happened, the more unlikely both of those explanations seem.

Why would a burglar come all the way from England to Seacliffe, Massachusetts, to break into a house that's lit up like there's a party going on?

And why isn't there any evidence of his breaking in?

And if he was a burglar, why was *he* afraid of *me*?

On the other hand, if he was a ghost, why was *he* so spooked when he saw *me*?

Besides, a ghost wouldn't need to take off running out of the house, right? All he'd have to do would be to fade, or vanish, or whatever ghosts do when they need to scram.

But if he wasn't a burglar . . .

And he wasn't a ghost . . .

Then who the heck was he?

I'm lying in bed, and I can't sleep.

Tonight, it's not because of the lack of street noise, or because I'm squeezed into a twin bed with my brother. Peter is down the hall in his own room. And I'm actually glad there's no street noise, and that the only thing I hear through my open window is crickets and, in the distance, the water.

It makes it easier for me to listen for footsteps in the yard—or someone breaking into the house again.

That's right. Here I am, playing watchdog, while the rest of my family is sleeping blissfully.

You probably thought I would tell my parents about the intruder.

You might have expected me to have called the Seacliffe police right away and report him, too.

But I didn't do either of those things.

And before you decide that I'm as nutty as the rest of the people in this town, let me explain.

I really thought about telling my parents.

In fact, I spent the whole rest of the time while they were still at the concert figuring out exactly what I was going to tell them.

I even looked forward to telling them. I kept imagining how they would say, "That does it! We're leaving this wretched place—it's not safe!" And then we'd all rush upstairs and pack our bags and peel out of the driveway in the Chevy.

That was such a perfect fantasy that I immediately knew there had to be a hole in it.

And of course, there was.

Because as soon as I tried to see things from my parents'
perspective, I realized what would happen.

After all, they know I hate it here. Why should they believe
me when I tell them someone broke into the house? Especially when there's no evidence of how he got in? Especially
when I tell them he looked like Ringo and was wearing a
pilgrim suit and I scared him away?

I mean, how would you react if someone told you a story
like that?

And even if I did tell my parents and they believed me,
what would happen? They'd call the police, and *they* wouldn't
believe me.

Or worse yet, everyone would believe me and my parents
would be so worried that they'd drive me crazy. They'd probably never leave me alone—they'd drag me to fife and drum
concerts every night, and if I refused to go, they might even
hire Mrs. Gramucci to come up here and baby-sit me.

And I would just die if Riley Kennedy found out I had to
have a baby-sitter.

So basically, I've decided to keep my mouth shut about
the entire episode. After all, whoever the intruder was, he
didn't seem dangerous. He had the perfect opportunity to
attack me, and what did he do? He ran away.

And I doubt if he'll ever come back.

There's no way he'd ever want to come back.

As long as I keep drilling that fact into my head, I'll be
fine.

FIVE

I must have finally drifted off to sleep at around three A.M. Sunday morning, my mother wakes me up at seven-thirty.

"Come on, Mom, let me sleep," I groan, but she's relentless.

"It's Father's Day," she says. "We're all going to church together, and after that, we're going out for breakfast to celebrate."

Oh, yeah. Father's Day. I almost forgot.

There's something else I almost forgot. The intruder.

Now, with sunlight shining in through the window, it seems as if last night didn't really happen.

Then I spot the umbrella next to my bed. I put it there so that it would be within reach in case of an emergency.

So it was real. Someone really was here last night.

Bleary-eyed, I get up and get ready. Not only do I do my hair in a flip and spray it firmly into place, but I try a new makeup trick I read about in a magazine. It said that if you use white makeup, your eyes will seem bigger. My eyes are my best feature—they're brownish gold and already are pretty big—so I guess playing them up can't hurt.

I also wear another new outfit—a mustard-colored sleeveless sheath with a matching brown sleeveless cardigan and pillbox hat. I bought it in the Young Sophisticates shop in

Gimbels. Naturally, I was imagining how Brian's eyes would light up when he saw me in it.

I don't know why I'm wearing it today. Even if I do happen to bump into Riley Kennedy, that fluffball Trudy will probably be hanging on his arm.

And besides, I have a boyfriend, so it doesn't matter what Riley thinks of me.

Still, I slide my feet into my new brown leather Baker pumps and squirt on some Joy perfume. My grandmother bought me a little bottle of it last Christmas. It costs fifty dollars an ounce and I usually save it for special occasions, but what the heck?

Then I have to hunt through my suitcase—which is still full of underwear and girdles and socks and bras that I haven't unpacked yet—for the Father's Day present I bought my dad at B. Altman last week. It's a tie. I always get him a tie—I can't think of anything else a father would like—anything I can afford on my baby-sitting salary, that is.

When I come downstairs, my mother is in the kitchen, pulling on her gloves. "You look very nice, Abbey," she tells me.

"So do you." She's wearing her favorite navy blue crepe suit and matching hat.

"We're going to be late," she tells me, then calls, "Frank? Boys? We have to go."

"What church are we going to?" I ask her. In New York, we go to a beautiful old stone one on Fifth Avenue. I always pass the time by counting the panes of stained glass in the windows.

"The one next to the movie theater on the commons," my mother says. "Mary Kennedy said the priest is wonderful."

Mary Kennedy. That must be Katie and Riley's mother.

"Today is a special service," my mother continues, examining her reflection in a compact mirror from her purse.

"For Father's Day?"

"No." She pats her hair into place, then puts the compact away. "It's a special historic commemoration, to go along with Puritan Days."

It just figures.

My father and the twins come into the kitchen then. All three of them look scrubbed and handsome in their Sunday suits.

"Happy Father's Day, Dad," I say, giving him a kiss on the cheek.

He hugs me. "Thank you, Abbey-my-girl. You look very pretty today. Is that a new dress?"

"Yup. Do you like it?"

"It's nice; but the colors are a little . . . dull, aren't they?"

"Dad! Deep earth tones are the newest look!"

"Is that right?" He looks dubious. Then he sniffs. "Mmm. Is that perfume I smell?"

"Uh . . . maybe."

He and my mother exchange a look. My father says to her, extra casually, "So, are the Kennedys going to be at this service?"

"I think so, Frank."

My father winks at me. "I take it you've met the young fella—Riley?"

I shrug and turn away because I feel my face growing hot. "Yes, I've met him. And he's an arrogant jerk."

"I see."

"Aren't we going to be late?" I ask crossly, heading for the door.

"Yes, let's go," says my mother, and we all go outside— just as the Kennedys are coming out of their back door.

Riley, I immediately notice, is wearing a dark suit. And he has a crew cut, and his hair is a brownish auburn color.

"Hi, Abbey!" Katie calls, waving cheerfully. I see that she's wearing a pink-and-white seersucker dress and a straw bowler-type hat—the kind I used to wear about five years ago.

I wave at her and continue walking toward our car, which is parked just across the low hedge from theirs.

Mr. Kennedy—a handsome man who looks like he once played football—starts giving my dad directions to the church, and Mrs. Kennedy and my mother exclaim over each other's hats. Peter and Paul are already in the car, each of them sitting by a window. Naturally I'll get the middle again.

"Hey, New *Yo-awk*," Riley calls over the bushes as I start to climb into the car. "Nice yellow dress."

"It's not yellow," I inform him frostily.

"It's not?" He squints at me. "Looks like yellow to me."

"It's mustard."

"Mustard? What are you, a hot dog?" He cracks up at his joke as he's getting into the backseat of their car with Katie, who swats his arm.

It strikes me as funny, too, but naturally, I don't give him the satisfaction. I just shoot him a haughty look and climb over Paul, who's laughing hysterically and keeps repeating "a hot dog!"

As we head to church, I tell myself that at least Riley noticed my dress.

The church is a white clapboard building with plain, glass-paned windows. It almost looks like a house, except for the steeple.

I scan the crowd of people on the sidewalk going in, looking for someone with long, shaggy hair. Then I wonder what I'll do if I spot the intruder, anyway. Holler, "stop, thief?"

On second thought, I doubt that he'd be in church, anyway. If he is a burglar, he's probably in some hideout, plotting his next crime.

And if he *isn't* a burglar, well . . . I don't really want to think about that anymore.

We sit in a pew behind the Kennedys. I spend the entire service fiddling with my Beatles medallion and staring at the back of Riley's head. I can't help noticing how his ears stick out and how tan the little patch of skin between the bottom of his crew cut and the top of his collar is.

I decide not to do this white makeup thing anymore, even if it does emphasize my eyes. It may be the latest style in New York City, but here on the Massachusetts coast, the golden bronzed look is where it's at. I'll have to start concentrating on getting a tan as soon as possible.

Anyway, everyone knows the sun is good for your skin. Maybe it'll help clear up this annoying patch of pimples that keeps popping up on my forehead.

After communion, the priest goes on and on about how this church was formed two hundred and seventy-one years ago, and how the first settlers of Seacliffe fled England so that they could have freedom to worship, and yada yada yada. Then the church choir sings a bunch of patriotic songs.

During "This Land Is Your Land," when they reach the line about "the New York Island," Riley turns his head and catches my eye. He flashes me that white-toothed grin.

And even though I already know he's an arrogant jerk, my stomach does a nervous little quivering number on me.

* * *

We're finally back home.

We went to a restaurant after church—this place called 1749 House. It's right on the town square and it was jammed with people. I guess all the churches let out at the same time. We had to wait for almost an hour to be seated, and by then, they had run out of their "world-famous blueberry pancakes." My brothers couldn't find anything else they wanted, so my mother had to talk the waitress into letting them order from the lunch menu, and by the time they fired up the broiler for the twins' hamburgers, we had been there for another hour.

Now I'm stretched out on a blanket in the backyard, listening to my transistor radio. I'm wearing my new tangerine-and-olive cotton plaid swimsuit. It's a two-piece with a strapless bra top for maximum tanning. Just to be sure, I coat myself with baby oil. Josie told me about that trick—she found out about it from her cousin. It's supposed to get you a fast, dark tan.

I don't know, though. I kind of feel like a french fry, lying out here sizzling in the sun. And little gnats and bugs keep flying into the oil slick on my arms and legs and getting trapped, which is thoroughly disgusting.

Still, Katie said something about going to the beach tomorrow, and I'm not about to show up there until I at least have some color.

The Kennedys drove right into Boston from church to spend Father's Day with their grandfathers, who live on the same block, according to Katie. She asked if I have any grandparents, and I told her about Grandpa Harmon in Florida. My mother's father, Grandpa Yates, died before I was even born.

"Abbey?" My mother pokes her head out the back door.

I sit up. "What?"

"We're going to go into town and walk around the park. The twins want Sno-Kones. Do you want to come?"

"No, thanks."

"Are you sure?"

"Positive."

I lie down again.

As soon as they're gone, everything seems really quiet. I turn up the volume on the radio, even though I'm not crazy about the station. It's the best one I can find, but they keep playing all of last year's hits, like "Locomotion" and "Soldier Boy."

After about an hour, "Johnny Angel" comes on.

I immediately remember that this is Trudy's favorite song. I really hate it.

I reach over and turn off the radio.

As soon as I lie down again, I hear something—a twig snapping, maybe—and it's come from the trees at the back of the property.

I sit straight up and look around.

There's nothing to see.

Everything is silent, except for chattering birds and the far-off sound of waves. Then a slight breeze stirs the air, rustling the leaves, and I think maybe that was what I heard. But I know that it wasn't. The sound was louder, and more sudden. Like the sound something—or someone—would make if they were creeping around in the woods right near the edge of our yard.

And as I stay absolutely still and listen, I get the eerie feeling that someone is hidden there among the trees, staring right back at me.

Despite the warm sun, the skin on my arms and legs suddenly feels taut and prickly with goose bumps. And my heart is starting to race.

That does it. I can't stand it. I jump up, grab the blanket and radio, and flee into the house.

After bolting the back door, I stand in the kitchen window for a long time, half expecting to see that peculiar intruder from last night lurking among the trees.

But he doesn't appear, and after awhile, I decide that I'm probably just doing a great job of spooking myself.

I'm on my way upstairs to get cleaned up when a shrill sound shatters the air. I'm so startled that I nearly lose my footing, and I have to grab the wooden bannister to keep from falling.

Then I realize that the sound is the telephone in the keeping room. It's ringing.

I hurry back down to answer it. "Hello?" I ask breathlessly.

"Abbey?"

"Yes. Mom? Where are you?"

"We're at Ted Leeworthy's house."

Who the heck is Ted Leeworthy? *"Where?"*

"He's the contractor who's going to help us with the remodeling, remember?"

I don't, but . . . "Yeah. What are you doing there?"

"We bumped into him and his wife at the park. They invited us back to their house for a barbecue. He lives in Salem and he has a son who's a year older than the twins."

"Oh."

"We'll be home around nine o'clock. There are cold cuts in the refrigerator for your supper. Have a sandwich and a can of soup. All right?"

"Fine," I murmur. All I can think is that I can't believe they aren't coming home until tonight. I'm going to be alone here for hours, and it's going to get dark. I should have gone with them to the stupid park. If I had, I'd be at Ted Leeworthy's house, too, instead of alone here in this creepy old place, scared out of my mind.

"Abbey?"

"Hmm?"

"Is everything all right?" My mother's voice sounds concerned.

I debate telling her that it's not all right. But then she'll ask what's wrong. And I'll have to tell her that I'm afraid to be alone.

"Everything's fine, Mom. See you later," I say brightly.

"All right. See you later."

"Okay. Bye."

I place the telephone receiver into its cradle and glance at the clock. It's almost four.

It'll probably stay light for at least a few more hours, I tell myself. And maybe my parents will have a boring time and come home early.

But what happens if it gets dark and I'm still all alone here—and *he* comes back?

You'd think that after a while, I would manage to calm down and realize there's nothing to be afraid of. You'd think *Sex and the Single Girl* would take my mind off of everything. You'd think so—but you'd be wrong.

I lie on my bed with my book, but I can't keep my mind on it. My thoughts keep drifting back to the stranger, and I can't shake this terrible sense of foreboding.

Finally, I snap the book closed and get up. I wander over to the window and stare out over the backyard. It's getting dark out.

Uh-oh.

Maybe I should go downstairs and turn on the television set.

That's a good idea. And I can make a sandwich, too. I

guess being petrified works up an appetite, because suddenly, I'm starving.

I feel better after turning on the television set and a few lamps in the keeping room. I can't turn on all the lights again—when my father came home last night, he was really mad that the house was all lit up. He gave his old, "What do you think, that I'm made of money?" speech.

In the kitchen, I get out the cold cuts and bread and lettuce and tomatoes and start making a sandwich. Just to prove to myself that everything's fine, I sing, "Love Me Do" as I slice the tomato.

I'm only a few lines into the song when I hear something outside.

Abruptly I stop singing and listen.

Nothing.

Frowning, still clutching the knife, I walk quietly over to the back door and peek out into the yard.

And that's when I see the shadow creeping away from the house.

SIX

I don't know what gets into me. But the moment I see the silhouette of a man in a broad-brimmed hat sneaking across the yard, toward the woods, I'm furious. I've had it.

I leap into action. Still holding the knife, I dash out the back door.

"Hey, wait!" I shout.

Startled, he glances over his shoulder, takes one look at me, and takes off.

And all I can think is that I can't let him get away.

Then, just before he reaches the cover of trees, he trips and goes flying to the ground. I'm right on top of him before he can get away.

That's when I realize what I've done. I must be insane. What do I think I'm doing, chasing a prowler around in the dark? It was an instinctive thing, a wild impulse. All that mattered was catching the intruder.

And now that I've got him, what am I supposed to do? He's bigger and stronger than I am. He could easily hurt me.

Then he looks up at me. And I see that he's petrified.

"No," he says in a voice that's barely above a whisper. And then I realize that he's staring at the knife, trembling.

I try to hold it steady so he won't see how badly my hand is shaking. "What are you doing here?" I ask, and my voice comes out booming.

He flinches. "I . . . Please, don't hurt me. I meant thee no harm."

I knew it! Didn't I guess that he was British? He has this really strong accent.

"Tell me what you're doing creeping around my house."

He doesn't reply, just stares up at me. His eyes are huge and he looks bewildered. I notice that he's unshaven and that there are scratches and smudges of dirt on his face.

And he's younger than I thought. He can't be much older than I am.

In the stillness, above the sound of chirping crickets, I can hear his heavy panting. He can't seem to catch his breath.

"Who are you?" I ask him, a little less forcefully.

Still, he doesn't reply.

"Tell me your name." It comes out like a command, and to reinforce it, I raise the knife a little. As long as he doesn't know that I would never be able to use it, I'll be fine.

" 'Tis Zachariah Wellbourne," he finally says in a low voice.

"Zachariah Wellbourne?" I repeat.

He nods mutely.

"What were you doing here?"

He looks away, and sees his hat lying close by. It fell off his head when he stumbled. I can tell he wants to reach for it, but he's afraid to make a move.

"What were you doing here?" When that still doesn't get a reply, I try, "Where do you live?"

He shifts his eyes back to mine and seems to be hesitating. Finally, he says, "Seacliffe."

"And what are you doing here, sneaking around in the dark?"

Instead of answering me, he shifts his gaze downward,

slowly, staring at me. He's looking me over from head to toe. Pervert.

"Why are you dressed that way?" I ask, to divert his attention.

Now his dark eyes snap back up to meet mine, and he seems defiant when he goes, "I might ask thee the same question."

I narrow my gaze at him. "What's that supposed to mean?"

He has some nerve to suggest that I'm the one who's dressed oddly. I'm the one wearing shorts, a T-shirt, and Keds. *He's* the one in the ruffled blouse and knickers. I can imagine what Brian and his friends would do to this guy if he showed up at our school in this getup.

When he doesn't respond, I say, "Listen, Bub, I'm sick and tired of everyone in this stupid town and all of your 'historic' this and 'historic' that. Get with the program and stop living in the past. I mean, this is 1963, not sixteen-whatever, and I don't know why you all can't . . ."

I trail off. He's made a hideous gasping noise and suddenly his eyes are bulging out of his face.

I'm about to ask if he's all right when he says, in a strangled voice, "What . . . please . . . repeat that . . ."

"What? I *said,* get with the program. You people in Seacliffe are so—"

"No! Not that. What year is it?"

Something in his tone makes me hesitate. A little chill begins to descend over me, and my eyes are as wide as his as I say slowly, "1963. What—what year did you think it was?"

It takes a moment for him to find his voice. And when he finally does, all he says, in a whisper, is, "1693."

"What?" I take a step backward. For the briefest moment,

I'm struck by the horrible realization that maybe this guy is for real.

Then I get a grip on myself. What was I thinking? Obviously, he's some nut who's taking this Puritan Days stuff way too seriously.

Suddenly, we both hear it—the sound of a car crunching in the gravel at the foot of the driveway beside the house.

Before I realize what's happening, he's scrambled to his feet and taken off into the woods as headlights are sweeping up the driveway.

I'm so confused that for a moment I don't move. Then I glance down and see his hat lying on the grass. Impulsively, I snatch it up and hurry into the house just before my father turns off the engine.

"Hi, Mrs. Kennedy, I'm sorry it's so early but is Katie up yet?" The words spill out in a rush, then I just stand there on their porch, staring at her.

"Why, Abigail, how lovely to see you. Please do come in," she says graciously. "Of course Kathleen is up. She's eating her breakfast."

I follow her through the house to the kitchen, where I see that Katie isn't the only one eating breakfast. Riley's sprawled in a chair next to her, chomping Special K and reading the cereal box.

Both he and Katie glance up, obviously surprised to see me.

Katie says cheerfully, "Good morning, Abbey!" She's fresh as a petunia in a pastel green sundress with a matching headband holding her smooth blond hair back from her scrubbed, rosy face.

"Uh, hi."

"Well, if it isn't Miss New Yo-*awk,*" Riley says, grinning. "Looks like you got yourself a sunburn."

He's right about that. I'm pink all over from yesterday, and I feel my face grow even hotter as Riley looks at me.

Maybe this wasn't such a good idea. It seemed like it was last night, when I was lying awake unable to sleep, wondering what to do. I thought that maybe Katie could shed some light on the strange boy, whose name I can't seem to remember for the life of me.

But now that I'm actually here in the Kennedys' kitchen, I'm not so sure.

"Won't you sit down, Abigail?" Mrs. Kennedy asks. "Would you like some orange juice?"

"No, thanks."

"Some cereal?"

"Or a cup of co-*awfee?*" Riley contributes.

I shoot him what I hope is a withering look. He just bobs his eyebrows at me and goes back to his cereal.

"No, thanks," I say to Mrs. Kennedy as I slide into the chair next to Katie's.

She swallows a mouthful of cereal before asking, "What have you been up to, Abbey?"

"Not much." I glance over at her mother, who's washing dishes at the sink and humming to herself.

"Did you bring that record over? We can play it if you like."

"No, I, uh, forgot it."

"Well, I'm done eating." She puts down her spoon and pushes back her chair. "Why don't we go back to your house and get it?"

"Um, actually, I really want to talk to you about something," I say in a low voice.

Riley looks up, interested.

"Not *you*," I tell him. "Katie."

"Really? What about?" Katie asks, clearly pleased that I want to confide in her.

I give Riley a pointed look. "In private," I say to her.

"Oh! All right. We can go up to my room." She pushes back her chair and carries her cereal bowl and empty glass over to the sink, where her mother cheerfully takes it and continues washing and humming.

"Come on," Katie says, heading out of the kitchen.

I toss a look over my shoulder at Riley, who's obviously intrigued. I notice that his hair looks damp and he has a tiny patch of tissue stuck to the side of his cheek, where he obviously cut himself shaving.

And despite my preoccupied frame of mind, I'm impressed. I know for a fact that Brian doesn't shave yet. He's got a baby face—but a *handsome* baby face, I remind myself firmly. I just can't seem to picture it very well at the moment. Riley's face keeps getting in the way.

I banish all thoughts of him from my head and follow Katie up the stairs.

Her room is exactly what I expected.

Pink flowered wallpaper. White painted woodwork.

Basically, the room looks like a magazine picture, with not one item out of place. It even smells good—like perfume and flowers and fresh air.

There's a canopy bed covered with frilly white eyelet that matches the ruffly curtains in the windows. There's a pink-skirted dressing table covered with toiletries, and a big floral print chair, and an old-fashioned bureau with a fancy carved mirror. In one corner is an elaborate dollhouse and a miniature antique baby carriage filled with dolls.

There are shelves along one entire wall. The top one's lined with stuffed animals. The others are full of books—the

Nancy Drew and Little House series, plus old classics like *Little Women* and *Five Little Peppers* and a few lame teen romances by Rosamund du Jardin.

I imagine what Katie would say about *Sex and the Single Girl*.

I think about my room in the house next door. My clothes are stacked everywhere because I still can't bring myself to put them into the musty old dresser drawers. And my suitcase is still filled with undergarments and sitting wide open in the middle of the floor.

Katie closes the door behind us, then turns around. I can tell she's bursting with anticipation. "Well? What is it?" she asks in her bubbly voice.

I hesitate. "Well . . ."

"Is something wrong?"

"Not really. It's just. . . . Something weird happened . . ." She's waiting expectantly.

I start again. "I probably shouldn't even think it's a big deal. I mean, you'll think I'm crazy. Actually, it's nothing."

"Come on, Abbey, obviously it's something."

"Okay." I take a deep breath. "Some guy broke into our house the other night, but I scared him away. And then last night, I caught him creeping around outside. And he—"

"Someone broke into your house? You have to call the police!"

I blink. "What?"

"Didn't you call them?"

I instantly regret that I ever decided to tell her. What was I thinking?

"Uh, never mind." I start moving toward the door. "Forget I said anything."

I reach for the knob, jerk the door open—and scream.

Riley is standing there, as startled to see me as I am to see him.

"What are you doing, Riley?" Katie demands, coming up behind me. "Are you eavesdropping?"

"Of course not!" But he's looking a little sheepish for a change.

"You were so." I glare up at him. "And you scared the heck out of me, too."

"Yeah. I'm telling Mom," Katie informs him.

Riley recovers some of his swagger. "Oh yeah? What are you going to tell her?"

"That you were standing outside my door eavesdropping."

"Prove it. I was just walking by. Can't a guy—"

"You are a pain, Riley Kennedy!" Katie cuts him off, closing her door in his face. She looks at me. "I'm sorry about that."

"It's okay."

But it isn't. And now I'm trapped. I can't leave with Riley lurking out in the hallway.

Katie goes over to the record player near the window. "I'll turn this on so he won't hear us," she tells me. She flips open a box of 45's and hunts through them before making a selection. She puts it on the turntable and lowers the arm.

"Johnny Angel" fills the air. Great. Just great.

"All right," Katie goes, flopping down onto her bed. "Tell me about the break-in."

"First you have to swear not to tell anyone. I mean, not *anyone*."

She holds up two fingers solemnly.

"What's that?"

"Girl Scout's honor."

Oh, sheesh. "Just promise you'll keep your mouth shut, okay?" I say impatiently.

"Okay."

"Because I haven't told anyone about this yet."

"Okay."

"I didn't go to the police because this wasn't just any break-in."

I take a deep breath, then start talking. And the whole story tumbles out. All of it, right down to the fact that the stranger thought it was 1693.

After keeping everything bottled up inside, it's an incredible relief to tell someone. Even if that someone is Katie Kennedy.

She doesn't say a word the whole time I'm talking. And when I'm done, her blue eyes are so wide they're bulging.

"He has to be a ghost!" is the first thing she blurts when she finds her voice.

I shake my head. "Uh-uh. He was real."

"How do you know? Ghosts can *look* real."

"I have his hat," I remind her. "And it's definitely real." I examined it thoroughly enough. I spent hours last night just clutching it and turning it over and over in my hands, looking for—I don't know what. There was no tag, nothing but rough black felt material inside and out.

"Where's the hat now?"

"Under my bed."

"Let's go look at it."

"Why?"

"It's a clue," she says with exaggerated patience, as if I'm an idiot.

She's really starting to get on my nerves again. I give her the evil eye. "Who are you, Nancy Drew?"

"Come on, Abbey. Can't you remember what he said his name was? Think hard."

"I *am* thinking hard. I've always been really bad with

names, Katie. I just can't remember. It was something old-fashioned."

"Miles?" she suggests.

I shake my head.

"Ambrose? Silas? Ezra? Phineas?"

"Phineas?" I echo, frowning at her. "Where the heck are you getting these names from?"

"Don't you ever read about history?"

"No, in New York we like to live in the present," I zing back at her.

Unfazed, she just says, "So, is it Phineas, or not?"

I shake my head impatiently.

This goes on for a few minutes—Katie spewing ridiculous, archaic names and me vetoing them. I'm about to tell her to shut up already when something jars my memory.

"What did you say?"

"Josiah?" she repeats hopefully.

I ponder it, then shake my head slowly. "No."

"But something like that."

"Maybe." I close my eyes and think as hard as I can. For once, Katie is silent.

Finally, I give up and open my eyes. "I just can't remember, Katie."

She looks disappointed. "Well, let's go to the library. It opens at nine."

"Why?"

"So that people can get there early. Sometimes there's even a line waiting."

Do you believe this girl? I say evenly, through gritted teeth, "Not *why* doesn't it open at nine. I meant, why do you want to go there?"

Now she's looking at me like *I'm* the lump head. "So that we can do research," she informs me. "They have all kinds of books and documents about local history. And they're on display this week because of the festival."

"But what are we going to research?"

She shrugs. "The history of the Crane house, and Seacliffe. Whatever."

The flushed, excited expression on her face is really annoying me. And spending the morning in the library studying local history with Katie is just about the last thing I want to do.

I shake my head and stand up abruptly. "That's all right, Katie. Let's go to the beach instead."

"The beach? Why?"

"Because I haven't been there yet and it's a nice day. And to tell you the truth, suddenly I'm sick of thinking about this whole intruder thing."

But Katie's not. I can tell by the look on her face. She's just itching to go do research.

"Or," I suggest casually, "I could just go to the beach by myself, if you don't want to come." *Please-please-please don't come,* I beg her silently.

"You wouldn't mind?"

I shake my head. "No, it's all right. Maybe we can get together later," I add, remembering that I do still want to play my Beatles record.

"Sure. You can come over and bring that record of yours. I really want to hear it." One point for her. "And the hat—it's an important clue," she adds.

Subtract that point.

"Right." I walk over to the door and yank it open, half expecting to see Riley crouched there. But the hallway is empty.

"So I'll see you later, all right?" I say to Katie.

"All right." She's wearing a bemused, faraway expression.

Good, I think as I go down the polished staircase and head for the front door. *Let her worry about it for a while.*

I feel better already, just having unloaded the story on someone. Now I just want to forget the whole thing ever happened.

cover, I think as I go inside the polished staircase and head
for the front door. And the song about the waltz—
g a song about a waltz, just saying, reminded me story, the
someone's dance. Her want to forget the whole thing ever
happened.

SEVEN

When I get home, I find my mother in the kitchen. Her hair is hidden beneath a scarf. She's wearing dungarees, which is rare for her, and standing on a chair doing something to the front of the cupboards.

"Oh, hi, Abbey," she says when I walk in. "Did you have a nice visit with Katie?"

"Uh-huh." I open the refrigerator and take out an apple, then bite into it and look up at her. "Mom?"

"Hmm?"

"What are you doing?"

"I'm stripping this wood," she says. "We're going to re-finish it."

"Oh. Where's Dad?"

"He took the twins to day camp, and then he's got to go to the hardware store. We're going to rip away the front steps today."

I take another bite of my apple. "How come?"

"Because they're rotting away."

If you ask me, the whole house is rotting away. I don't know why they're bothering to try to fix it up.

I wander upstairs to my room and stand in the doorway, surveying the mess. I really should find someplace to put my clothes.

I go over and sniff one of the dresser drawers. Maybe it

is aired out a little. I guess I might as well put my stuff inside. I can't very well leave my wardrobe in piles all over the room for the entire summer, can I?

For the next hour, I concentrate on putting things away.

And the whole time, I'm aware of that hat beneath my bed, even though I can't see it. I keep wondering about the boy who lost it. Where did he spend the night? Where is he now?

I know I should be angry at him for breaking into our house and creeping around outside. But instead, I find myself feeling sorry for him. Something tells me he's not dangerous, and that he has a good reason for wanting to get into this house.

A sudden knocking sound makes me jump.

The door opens a crack. "Abbey?" My father pokes his head inside.

"Yeah?"

"I picked up the mail from the post office box in town. You got a postcard."

"Already?" We left New York on Friday, and it's only Monday.

Eagerly, I grab the card from my father and see that it's a picture of the New York skyline. It *has* to be from Brian.

But it's not. It's from Josie.

"Thanks, Dad," I say, trying not to seem too disappointed.

"You bet." He closes the door and goes whistling down the hall.

The back of the card is covered with Josie's scrawl.

Hi Abbey—
You're not even gone yet and I miss you already. I
thought I'd send you this picture of the city in case you
get homesick. I'll keep an eye on Brian for you while

*you're away, okay? Please write me soon. This is going
to be one boring summer! Well, see ya!*

*Y.F.A.
Josie*

Y.F.A.—that's "your friend always." I read the card over
again. And then again.

Suddenly, I'm miserable. Why do I have to be stuck here
in this stupid town so far away from home for the whole
summer?

I swallow back a lump of misery and toss the card onto
my bed, next to the clothes that still need to be put away.

I'm no longer in the mood, but I guess I might as well
hurry up and get it over with.

Since there's no closet, I have to hang the dresses and
things on this old wardrobe rack in the corner. Everything
is pretty wrinkled, but there's no way I'm going to iron right
now.

Finally, I'm finished.

It's almost noon.

Going to the beach has lost its attraction, but what else
am I going to do with myself all day?

Sighing, I open a drawer and take out my bathing suit.

It takes me almost a half hour to walk to the beach. That's
because I'm too chicken to take the shortcut through the
woods at the back of our property. You never know if that
intruder is still lurking there.

By the time I reach the sign that says SEACLIFFE TOWN
BEACH, I'm sweltering hot. The sand is pretty crowded, and
I look around for a place to put my blanket. There seems to
be an empty spot right in front of the lifeguard tower, so I

head in that direction, telling myself that, of course, I'm not hoping to bump into Riley or anything. It just happens to be the only free area.

But as I get closer to the weathered wooden stand, I squint through my sunglasses to see if he happens to be on duty.

The lifeguard has his back to me as he looks out over the water. But the short auburn hair and the cocky way he's twirling his whistle on a string are a dead giveaway.

It's Riley, all right.

And he's not wearing a shirt. His shoulders and back are broad and muscular and a deep bronze color. Not that I'm looking on purpose. But you can't really miss him.

That doesn't mean I have to acknowledge his presence or anything. And I don't plan to.

I arrive at the empty patch of sand in front of his stand and spread my blanket out. The wind keeps whipping the edges, so it isn't easy. I kick off my sandals and use them to weigh down two corners. Then I sit and shimmy out of my shorts. Casting them aside, I lift my T-shirt over my head.

Instantly, there's a whistle from above.

I look up to see Riley grinning down at me. His eyes are hidden behind black sunglasses.

"Hey, New Yo-*awk*," he says, waving. "How ya doin'?"

I just shrug and take off my sunglasses, tossing them onto the blanket. Then I stand up and take off for the water.

I pause at the edge and wonder why hardly anyone else is actually swimming. They're all just wading around up to their knees.

The water seems cleaner than it is at Rockaway, which is the only place I've ever gone swimming in the ocean. Josie's uncle has a house there.

So if the water's clean, why isn't anyone swimming in it?

I'll show these dullards what you're supposed to do at the beach.

The moment I make the mistake of diving right in, I realize what the problem is.

The water is so icy that my entire body instantly becomes one giant ache.

I come up sputtering, glance out of the corner of my eye, and see Riley watching. He even waves.

I lift one numb arm and wave back.

Naturally, I try to act like I'm enjoying myself immensely in the frigid ocean. I promise myself that as soon as he looks away, I'll get the heck out of here.

But he doesn't look away.

Of course, he's just doing his job. He's *supposed* to keep an eye on swimmers, in case someone starts drowning. And since I'm the only idiot stupid enough to actually be swimming, he's keeping an extra careful eye on me.

But he seems to be enjoying it.

It's probably just my imagination.

Or maybe, knowing him, he thinks I won't be able to swim.

I hate to admit it, but I show off a little for his benefit. I happen to be a good swimmer, compliments of four years of lessons at the neighborhood Y.

But after about five minutes of forced frolicking, I've had it. I'm practically paralyzed with cold.

I don't care if Riley is watching. I make my way back to the warm sand.

"Hey, you city girls are real hardy types, huh?" Riley calls down to me when I arrive at my blanket and snatch up my warm towel.

My teeth are chattering too violently for speech, so I just shrug and turn my back. Then I plop down on the blanket and pray for the beaming sun to do its job.

I'm so intent on warming up that I don't see Riley until he sits down next to me.

"Hi," he says casually.

"Hi." I avert my eyes from his sculpted bare chest and try to stop shivering.

"Cold?"

"Nope."

"Your lips are purple," he observes.

I scowl at him. "Aren't you supposed to be saving lives or something?"

"I'm on break."

I glance over my shoulder and see that some other guy has replaced him on his wooden perch.

"So how do you like the beach?" Riley asks, stretching out his tanned, muscular legs along the blanket. The hair on them is curly and bleached blond from the sun.

"The beach? It's fine."

"You don't have beaches like this where you live, huh?"

"For your information," I say frostily—which is easy, given my current body temperature, "we have better beaches."

"Oh, yeah? Where?"

"Rockaway, for one. And the water doesn't cause instant paralysis there, either."

He flashes a triumphant look at me through his dark glasses. "I knew you were cold."

"I am not."

"You are so." He leans closer and goes, in a low voice, "I bet I could warm you up pretty fast."

"I just bet you could," I say, looking him in the eye.

He raises his eyebrows.

Then I realize in horror that I'm flirting with him.

What's the matter with me? I've got a boyfriend back

home. Poor Brian is probably pining away for me right this very minute.

I tear my eyes away from Riley's and look out over the water.

So does he, but I know he's plotting. I can just feel it.

"What are you doing tomorrow night?" Riley asks nonchalantly after a pause.

See? I told you.

"Me?" I look back over at him.

"Yes, you."

"Why?" I ask suspiciously.

"Because I want to take you out."

I can't help it. The way he says it, in that totally straightforward way, turns me on. I get little goose bumps all over, and they're not just from being cold.

Then I think, *Brian.*

Coming to my senses, I try to appear offended. I say, "I can't go out with you, Riley," as though it's the craziest thing I've ever heard.

He's obviously surprised. "Why not?"

"Because I have a boyfriend."

He looks around. "Where?"

"Not here—back home."

"Oh." He ponders that for a moment, then shrugs. "Well, the way I see it, he's there, and you seem to be here. And so am I."

"That's not the way I see it."

Apparently, this makes no difference to him, because he just goes, "So how about it?"

"How about what?" I sound like Katie, but then, he's probably used to that.

"How about going out with me?"

Instead of saying no, as I fully intend to do, I find myself saying, "Where would we go?"

He's ready with an answer. "I have two tickets to the pageant tomorrow night."

"What pageant?"

"Haven't you heard about it? It's for Puritan Days. It's a historical—"

"No, thanks," I interrupt. "I can't go."

"Why not?"

"Because I have a *boyfriend,*" I tell him.

I can't believe I almost considered cheating on Brian.

Riley looks disappointed. "Are you sure?"

"Am I sure I have a boyfriend? Yes." *Even if I can't seem to picture his face at the moment.*

"Oh, well, I tried." Riley stands up. "Let me know if you change your mind."

"I won't."

"You might." He points to the snack bar across the way. "I'm going over there to get some lunch. Want to come?"

"No, thanks."

"I didn't think so. Well, see ya, New Yo-*awk.*"

"See ya."

I watch him walk across the sand. He's about ten yards from me when a curvy brunette in a two-piece bathing suit falls into step with him.

I abruptly turn away.

I spend the next five minutes soaking up the sun and trying to relax and think pleasant thoughts. But it's not working.

I keep thinking of Riley.

And when I command myself to stop thinking of him, my mind drifts to the stranger in the old-fashioned clothes.

Finally, I stand up and shake out my towel.

This day at the beach is no day at the beach.
I might as well go home.

When I get back to the house, I find two workmen and my father ripping away the wooden steps in front of the door.

"Abbey-my-girl," my father calls when he spots me walking up the driveway. "You had a phone call while you were gone."

"I did?" It must have been Brian.

"Yup. Josie called and your mother told her you were at the beach—Here, Joe, try this," he says, handing one of the workmen a bigger crowbar. "Anyway," he says, turning back to me, "she said it was important."

"Can I call her back, Dad? I'll pay for the long distance charge out of the baby-sitting money I saved up." I have about twenty-five dollars stashed in the toe of one of my shoes upstairs.

"She said she'll call you back," my father says, grabbing a piece of wood that goes flying as Joe tackles a new portion of the steps.

"When?"

"Later. She was going shopping, I think—Whoa, there, Clarence, let me get that for you." He leaps over some boards to help the other workman.

I walk around back and into the house, wondering what was so important Josie would call me long distance. We had agreed that we'd have to rely on letters to stay in touch all summer. Josie's always flat broke, and she told me that if I was going to call anyone long distance, she'd understand if it was Brian. She's a terrific friend, isn't she?

In the kitchen, the cupboards look worse than they did before my mother started stripping them, whatever that

means. They used to be painted white, at least. Now they're
all bare and patchy-looking.

Mom is at the sink, scrubbing her hands. "Hi, sweetheart.
How was the beach?"

"It was all right."

"Josie called. She said—"

"I know, Dad told me."

"Is he almost finished out there?"

I shrug. "I can't tell."

"Oh, and Katie Kennedy stopped over, too. She said to
tell you she got a baby-sitting job for this afternoon and
tonight. She'll talk to you tomorrow morning."

"Okay."

"She's such a sweet girl."

"Isn't she just."

My mother nods and smiles. Sarcasm is almost always
lost on her. She shuts off the water and dries off her hands.
"What do you think of the cupboards?"

I look at them, then back at her, and lie. "They look great."

"Well, they will after I'm through with them," my
mother says. "The whole house is going to be beautiful.
See that doorway?" She gestures at the narrow passage
leading from the keeping room into the kitchen. "We're
going to knock out the cupboard next to the fireplace in
there and make the archway wider. And then we're going
to knock out that broom closet over there and open things
up so that—"

"That's nice, Mom," I interrupt. I know it's rude, but my
eyes are glazing over. I could care less what they're going
to do to this house. All I want to do is get out of here and
go back home.

* * *

When the phone rings after supper, I snatch it up. I've been sitting right next to it for most of the afternoon and evening, writing letters to Brian and Siobhan and waiting for Josie to call back. The phone happens to be right near a window that looks out over the Kennedys' driveway.

About a half hour ago, Riley came out and started shooting baskets at the hoop nailed to their garage. I've been trying to ignore him, but it isn't easy. And if you ask me, he knows I'm here, even though he hasn't acknowledged me. He's showing off with all these fancy dribbling moves.

Now I focus all my attention on the voice on the other end of the telephone wire.

"Ab'? Is that you?"

"It's about time, Josie! I've been waiting to hear from you for hours!"

"Sorry. I went down to the sale at Best and Company with my sister. And then after that, she dragged me to the Young Flair department at B. Altman."

"Did you buy anything?"

"Are you kidding? I have ten cents to my name. In fact, I set my mother's egg timer so that I can keep this phone call short. It's going to cost a fortune, but it was an emergency."

"What? Is everything all right? Did something happen to someone?"

"Not exactly . . ." Josie sounds hesitant, which isn't at all like her. She usually talks a mile a minute.

"What is it, Jo?" A horrible thought strikes me. "Oh, God, it's Brian, isn't it? Something happened to Brian."

"It's Brian, but . . ." She trails off again.

"Oh, no!" I feel like I'm going to throw up. "Tell me. Was he in an accident?"

"No!" she goes quickly. "Nothing like that."

"Then what?"

There's a pause, then a sudden shattering ringing sound blasts into my ear. I jump out of my chair. "What was that, Josie?"

"The egg timer. I told you I had to keep this short."

"Then hurry up and tell me. What happened?"

"Well, I was at the movies last night with Rhonda Karminski—we went to see *Cleopatra*. By the way, it wasn't that great, have you seen it?"

"No. *What about Brian?*" I ask through gritted teeth.

"Ab', are you sitting down?"

I plop back into the chair. "Yes."

"There was this really boring part in the middle of the movie, so I decided to get some popcorn. And just as I was coming up the aisle and noticing this couple in the back row making out all hot and heavy, they came up for air. Ab', it was Brian."

"*What?* Are you sure?"

"Of course I'm sure. He was with Kiki Lindstrom. Remember her? The blonde from that party we went to in Queens?"

"You bet I remember her. I *knew* she was after Brian. I knew it! That rat fink! I haven't even been gone a whole week! How could he—"

"Listen, Abbey, I hate to do this, but I have to hang up."

"Josie, wait!"

"Ab', I can't. I don't know how I'm going to pay for this as it is. And there's really nothing more to tell."

"Okay, okay, go ahead. Thanks for calling me."

"What are you going to do?"

"I have no idea."

"Well, I'm sorry I had to be the one to tell you. But anyway, I miss you lots and I can't wait till you're back."

"Me either." But suddenly, I'm not as anxious as I was.

Why would I want to be in the same town as that two-timing Brian Burleigh and his new blond cuddle bunny?

"I have to go now, Abbey. 'Bye . . ."

" 'Bye, Josie. Take care."

"You too."

"And thanks."

"No problem. See ya."

And she hangs up.

Fuming, I just sit there for a minute. I can't believe that the whole time I've been moping around and missing Brian, he's been scheming and cheating. I can't believe I ever trusted him. The moment I left home he must have—

A thumping sound outside distracts me. I glance out the window. It's dusk now, but I can plainly see Riley dribbling up for a hook shot. The basket sails neatly through the hoop and I hear him shout, *"Yes!"*

And suddenly, I know exactly what I'm going to do.

I march out the back door and cut through the dividing hedge before I have time to think twice about it.

"Hey," I call to Riley, who's dribbling the ball under his leg with his back to me.

He stops dribbling, turns around, and looks surprised to see me. "What's going on, New Yo-*awk?* Want to play one-on-one?" He tosses me the ball.

I impulsively catch it, noticing how much more mature Riley, who's eighteen, looks and sounds compared to Brian, who's two months younger than me. "Not really."

"Then what?" He takes a few steps closer. I see the sweat dripping down his tanned, handsome face. He's slightly out of breath and I can see his broad chest heaving up and down under his white T-shirt.

"I have a question for you."

"Shoot."

"This?" I hold up the ball.

Yes, I'm flirting. So what?

He grins and wipes sweat from his forehead with the back of his hand. "You can shoot that if you want, too, but I meant the question."

I take a deep breath, then blurt, "Is that offer still open? About that pageant, or whatever, tomorrow night?"

Now he really looks surprised—and pleased. "Yeah. Why?"

"I'll go," I say quickly, then throw the ball into his hands. He misses and it goes bouncing across the concrete.

"Better get that," I say, motioning, then turn and head for the house as Riley goes after the ball.

"Hey!" he calls as I put my hand on the knob. "Abbey!"

He's never called me that before. I like the way it sounds coming from him. I turn around. "Yeah?"

He's got the ball under his arm and he's standing there looking at me. "How come you changed your mind?"

"I happen to like historical pageants," I say with a shrug, then hurry into the house.

EIGHT

"Abbey? Are you awake?"

"No!" I grunt and roll over. The room is dark.

I hear footsteps on the wooden floor of my room and my mother's voice comes closer. "Abbey, it's after nine o'clock."

"It can't be. It's still dark," I mumble.

"It's raining out, that's why. Katie Kennedy is downstairs waiting for you."

My eyes pop open. "Why?"

"She says she needs to talk to you."

I yawn and stretch. "Tell her I'll talk to her later."

"Abigail Harmon, you get out of this bed. You have a guest and it would be very rude not to come down and see her."

"I think it's very rude to drop by someone's house at the crack of dawn," I retort.

My mother narrows her eyes at me. "It isn't the crack of dawn. Get up, Abigail. Now!"

Reluctantly, I do. But I take my sweet time washing up and getting dressed. I even make my bed, which is something I usually only do when my parents force me.

When I finally show up in the kitchen, Katie's sitting at the table nibbling an Oreo and talking to my mother, who's spreading some kind of stain on the cupboards with a paintbrush. As usual, Katie's decked out in a pastel dress and matching ribbon in her ponytail.

The minute she catches sight of me, she pops the rest of the Oreo into her mouth and jumps up. "Here's Abbey now. Well, it was nice chatting with you, Mrs. Harmon." She grabs a stack of books from the table. "Come on, Abbey, let's go up to your room."

Before I can protest, she's on her way into the keeping room and heading toward the stairs.

"Hey, wait a second!" I catch up to her. "What's going on?"

"We have to talk," she whispers, holding a finger to her lips and continuing to the stairs.

Frowning, I overtake her and lead the way to my room.

"This is such a great room," she says when she steps inside. I scowl. "It is not."

At least it's not a total mess, now that my clothes are put away and the bed is made.

The rain is pattering on the roof above our heads, and the room is gloomy and dark. I turn on the lamp by the bed.

"Sure it's a great room," Katie says, looking around. "You get to have a fireplace . . . and all these great antiques. I just love the bed." As if to accentuate that statement, she plops down onto the mattress, which is the new one that was delivered on Saturday.

"Make yourself at home," I say dryly.

"Thanks. Where's the hat?"

For a second, I honestly don't know what she's talking about. I've been so preoccupied with the whole Brian-Kiki business, not to mention the fact that I somehow seem to have a date with Riley tonight, that I almost forgot about the intruder and everything.

And now that it all comes back to me, I'm not really in the mood to deal with it. "Oh, the hat's around somewhere," I say vaguely.

"Can I see it?"

I look at her and realize she's going to push this thing until I show her, so I might as well make it easy on myself. I crouch down and retrieve it from beneath my bed.

"Wow," she breathes, as if she's in awe. "Can I touch it—or hold it?"

"Here. Knock yourself out," I say, handing it over.

She takes it tentatively and runs her hands over the black felt. Then she sniffs it. "This is really something," she announces, her blue eyes wide. "It even smells like it's really old."

I roll my eyes.

Katie doesn't notice. "I couldn't wait to talk to you today," she says. "I went to the library yesterday and checked out all of these," and she pats the stack of books beside her on the bed, "so that we could do some research."

I pick up the book on the top of the pile. *"Ghosts of New England.* What's this for?"

"I read it last night, after the kids I was baby-sitting went to sleep. Look on page 156—I folded the corner of the page down for you."

"Why?" I turn right to it.

"Read the paragraph halfway down the page. The one under the heading 'Seacliffe, Massachusetts.' "

I nod and start reading, but she protests, "No, aloud. I want to hear it, too."

"Didn't you already read it?"

"Yes, but come on, Abbey." She leans back on her elbows expectantly, still holding the hat in one hand.

Sighing, I start over. " 'Probably the most famous haunted sight in the coastal town of Seacliffe is the Crane house on Old Post Road. Built in 1685 by Josiah Crane, a local merchant, the dwelling was home to his eldest daughter Felicity Crane, who at the age of sixteen in 1692 was executed for practicing witchcraft. It was rumored that one of the Crane family's slaves, an island woman named Jemima, was responsible for bewitching the young girl. The slave had mysteriously vanished a short time before Felicity Crane was accused, and it was rumored that Josiah Crane had murdered her and hidden her body beneath the dirt floor of the house—' "

"See?" Katie interrupts excitedly. "Didn't I tell you?"

I just nod and go on. " 'The ghost of Jemima has been reportedly seen in the large keeping room of the house many times over the years. Because she had been spotted near the old fireplace in that room, there was speculation that her body might have been buried beneath the hearth. In 1895, Marcus Whaley, who owned the house, ripped up the floorboards in the keeping room and excavated the old dirt floor beneath. While the bones of the slave weren't found, the ghost has continued to haunt the room over the years.' " I look up at Katie. "That's it."

"So what do you think?" she asks.

"I think it's a pretty creepy story. But it doesn't tell me anything about the boy who broke in the other night."

"Didn't you say you first heard him in the keeping room?"

"Yes, but I already told you, Katie, I don't think he was a ghost. I thought you were going to research the history of Seacliffe, not ghost stories. And anyway, this book doesn't say anything about the ghost of a young man."

Katie just shrugs. She's still clutching the hat. "I know, but if there's one ghost lurking around, there are probably more."

I involuntarily shiver. "Oh, thanks a lot. I'm the one who has to live here. What are those other books about?"

"There's another ghost one, but it doesn't say anything

about Seacliffe. And these others are about the witchcraft trials and other local history." She holds up a thin blue-covered pamphlet that bears the title, *The History of Seacliffe, Massachusetts*. "This one's the best—it was written by the local historical society. I'll leave these all here with you— they're not due back until two weeks from yesterday."

I start to tell her I don't really want them, but she goes on, "And I think we should go to the historic pageant tonight, too. I heard it's going to be about the witchcraft trials."

I just stare at her. Obviously she doesn't know I'm already going with her brother. Suddenly, I feel funny about the whole thing.

"Uh, Katie . . ."

"Do you have an umbrella? I lost mine, and we'll need one. It's so lousy out, although this is nothing compared to some of the Nor'easters we get around here."

"Nor'easters?"

"They're really bad storms that blow in from the Northeast. But if you have an umbrella, we can walk into town and get tickets," she continues. "They sell them at a booth in the park. And then—"

"Katie!" I cut her off.

She looks taken aback. "Yes?"

"I'm already going to the pageant."

"You are? With your family?"

"Um, no." I clear my throat. "With Riley."

She stares at me. "Riley?"

"Yes."

"My brother Riley?"

"How many Rileys do you know?"

"Three," she goes automatically. "Riley Jenkins, Riley O'Riley, and my brother."

"Did you say Riley *O'Riley?*" I ask, but she's too busy absorbing the idea of my date with her brother.

I fiddle with the binding on the ghost book, watching her. Finally, she looks at me and says, "I thought you had a boyfriend."

"Not anymore."

"How could that be? You haven't even seen him, have you? I thought he was back in New York."

"He is. But my best friend called me last night and told me he cheated on me."

"Oh." She ponders this for a moment, then looks me in the eye. "I don't mean to butt into your business, Abbey, but I think it's up to me to tell you that Riley isn't the best candidate for a boyfriend. He likes to play the field."

"I know. You already told me." I'm really feeling annoyed with her. "And who said I want a new boyfriend? All I'm doing is going out on a date with him."

Katie stands up. Her usually benign green eyes are flashing. I wonder what's with her.

"Well, don't come to me if you get hurt," she says. "And remember, I tried to warn you."

I stand up, too. "I won't. Because I'm not going to get hurt. I could care less what Riley does."

And that's the truth, I tell myself firmly. After all, I barely know him.

Katie shrugs, tosses the hat on the bed, and heads for the door. "Fine."

"Fine!" I call after her.

She doesn't look back, just walks out of my room and shuts the door behind her.

I sit on the bed and wonder what just happened. Obviously, my dating Riley is a sore spot with Katie. Well, it's too bad.

I tell myself that I don't care if she never speaks to me again.

But I know that's not true. She might be a pain in the neck, but I can't help feeling kind of bad.

Sighing, I peer out the window at the soggy world.

What am I going to do with myself all day?

"Abbey?"

I turn around. My mother is standing in the doorway.

"Yeah?" I say.

"Why did Katie leave so quickly?"

"I don't know. I guess she had to get home."

"Oh. Well, Daddy and I are going to drive into Boston. We have to see Great-Uncle William's lawyer about some paperwork for the house. We thought we'd stop for lunch, too. Do you want to come?"

"How long are you going to be gone?"

"The boys need to be picked up from camp at around four, so we'll be back before then. Why?"

"No reason." I'm not exactly thrilled about going out of town for the day—I want to have enough time to get ready for my date with Riley tonight. But I've been left alone in this house a few times too many. And for all I know, that strange boy is still lurking around somewhere. "All right, I'll go."

She looks pleased. "Good. And I was thinking we could have family night after supper. I'll make popcorn and we can play Monopoly."

"I can't."

She raises her eyebrows. "Why not?"

I really don't want to tell her, but I have no choice. "I—uh, I'm going out. To that historic pageant in town."

"With Katie?"

For a fleeting moment, I consider lying. But she'd probably find out. She usually does. "No," I say. "With Riley."

She looks surprised. "Riley Kennedy?"

I think of recycling the *How many Rileys do you know* line, but instead I just say, "Yeah."

"A date?"

"Of course not. We're just friends."

My mother looks dubious. I know she's not crazy about Brian, who has a mischievous aura that makes parents not trust him. But I thought she liked Riley. She seems to think the whole Kennedy family is all-American perfection.

"What's wrong?" I ask.

"I thought you were going steady with Brian Burleigh," is all she says.

I'm not about to go into that whole thing, so I just say, "I am. I told you, Riley is just a friend."

She nods and smiles at me. "He's a nice boy. Anyway, Daddy's waiting downstairs. Are you ready?"

"Sure." I follow her out of the room, wondering why everything always has to be so complicated these days.

It's still pouring rain when we leave Boston, and what should be a forty-five minute drive turns into nearly two hours.

It isn't a fun trip. My father always gets into a horrendous mood when he has to drive through traffic, and there's an ungodly amount of it in Boston. When my mother isn't shouting warnings at him like "Slow down!" or "Look out!" she's panicking about the twins, reminding my father that they'll be getting out of day camp at four, and can't he go any faster?

I just sit slumped in the backseat staring at the gloomy day, thinking about how Brian betrayed me and how I should be furious but for some reason I'm not. In fact, I'm secretly kind of glad, as much as I hate to admit it. Long distance relationships are too hard to keep up. And every time I start to acknowledge the thought that maybe I secretly wanted to go out with Riley all along, I push it away.

Finally, we're back in Seacliffe, and we go straight to the town hall. The day camp is held in the basement there on rainy days.

It's only ten after four when we get there, but all the other kids are gone. Peter looks worried and breaks into a relieved smile when we pop in the door.

Paul is unfazed that we're late—he's busy pestering a policeman who's smoking a cigarette on a bench in the hallway, asking him if he's ever shot a robber.

"Nah—there's no crime here in Seacliffe, sonny," the cop tells Paul good-naturedly.

Oh, sure, I think. *Did you know there's some prowler on the loose who thinks he's back in 1693?*

My mother practically has to pry Paul away from the guy, who says he's Officer Martell and looks flattered by the attention.

Paul has been fixated on policemen since he was just a little kid—he wants to be a cop when he grows up. That or a soldier.

You can just imagine how thrilled my mother is about that. She's always worrying that we'll be at war when the twins are old enough to be drafted, which isn't even until 1972.

My father tells her not to be ridiculous. He says America isn't stupid enough to get involved in another war—although even he was a little worried last October when we had that whole scare with the Cuban missiles. But as he pointed out, JFK got us out of that one, and he's going to keep us out of everything else, too.

My mother's only response to that is, "John Kennedy won't be in the White House forever."

Finally, we're driving back through the soggy streets toward home and I'm wondering what to wear for tonight. Riley said to be ready by six-thirty, which is only about two hours away.

"Whose truck is that?" Paul asks as we pull into the driveway.

It's raining so hard that for a moment I don't see anything. Then I notice that there's a big white panel truck parked near our back door.

"Joe Maccolini's," my father says. "He's the man who was working on the house yesterday. I told him to come over at around three-thirty. We have to take some measurements."

My father pulls our car to a stop next to the truck. Joe gets out just as we do, and we all duck and run through the rain.

I try to keep my hair from getting wet, but it doesn't work. Now it's going to take me forever to get ready.

In the kitchen, my father apologizes for being late.

"It's all right," Joe says. "You're lucky I got here on time, though, Frank. I caught someone prowling around your back door."

I was on my way out of the kitchen, but I stop dead in the doorway at Joe's words.

"You *what?*" my father asks.

"I pulled up in the driveway just in time to see someone fiddling around with the back door, like he was trying to get in."

My mother looks alarmed. So does Peter.

Paul says nonchalantly, "Don't worry. There's no crime in Seacliffe."

"All right, come on, boys," my mother says, snapping back

to her maternal, protective self. "Let's go upstairs and get you out of these wet clothes. You too, Abbey."

She ushers a protesting Paul and a frightened Peter out of the kitchen.

I remain rooted in the doorway. No one seems to notice.

"Did you catch him?" my father asks Joe, frowning.

"Nope. Soon as he saw my truck, he took off running for them woods out back. I tried to follow him, but the yard was so muddy that I kept slipping." Joe swipes at a rivulet of water that's running down his jowly face. "Couldn't even get a good look at him. It was too dark and rainy. All I know is that he was about six feet tall and kind of skinny. Oh yeah, and he was dressed all in black."

My heart feels like it's going to burst right out of my chest. I reach out and clutch the door frame to stay steady.

There's not a doubt in my mind who the prowler is.

He wants something.

Whatever it is, it's apparently in this house.

And it looks like he's going to keep coming back until he gets it.

NINE

I'm sitting next to Riley Kennedy in the dark junior high school auditorium, watching this production by the Seacliffe Theatrical Group.

I'll tell you one thing—it sure isn't *Oliver!* I saw that on Broadway with my drama club right before school got out, and everything about it was fantastic—acting, singing, sets, whatever.

On the other hand, this local yocal pageant is about the most boring thing I've ever seen. In fact, if it weren't for Riley's distracting presence, I'd probably be dozing off.

These people sure can't act. I could do a better British accent than most of them. Especially the narrator, a guy in a Puritan getup who occasionally steps forward to provide commentary in an annoying monotone.

The first half is all about how Seacliffe was settled back in sixteen-something by a bunch of Puritans from England. There's a whole melodramatic scene about coming over on a ship, and then this really long, boring part about electing someone to be in charge of the town.

Finally, it's time for intermission.

As soon as the lights come up, Riley turns to me and says, "Come on, let's go get something to drink in the lobby."

He follows me up the crowded aisle, but every time I turn around, he's lagging behind, saying hi to a different girl.

When he finally catches up, he goes, "Sorry. I keep seeing people I know."

"That's all right." I shrug as though I'm not completely jealous.

But I have to admit, he has been very attentive ever since he showed up at our door at six-thirty. And he looks so handsome tonight that I feel my belly do a little flip-flop whenever I look at him. He's wearing tan chinos and a creamy short-sleeved shirt that makes his tan stand out. And he smells good, too—like some kind of spicy lime aftershave.

Not only is he incredibly good-looking—and charming and relaxed, too—but he really knows how to treat a girl. He opens doors for me and that type of thing. Brian never used to do that. And I wouldn't have expected Riley to be the type, either. But he's really polite.

He's also sure of himself—not in an egotistical way, but in a way that tells you he doesn't worry about what other people think of him. It's very appealing.

And did I mention that he's a lot of fun?

He keeps making me laugh as we stand in the lobby drinking our punch. In fact, as intermission winds down, I feel like suggesting that we not stay for the second half. I wouldn't mind going to the drive-in restaurant out on the highway and just talking. But I don't have the nerve to suggest it.

And when Riley asks if I like the show so far, I say, "Oh, it's swell."

So we go back into the auditorium and the second half begins.

And as the narrator stands there in front of the curtain, droning on about the hard winter of 1691–1692, my mind wanders back, once again, to the disturbing news Joe told my father.

I can't believe that the prowler is still trying to get into our house.

I stare blankly at the stage as the curtain rises to reveal a flimsy cardboard backdrop. This whole thing—about the boy in the old-fashioned clothes, I mean—is really starting to scare me.

I'm afraid to think about it too deeply, to let myself explore the possibilities of who he is and where he came from. And I know I keep shoving those thoughts away because I'm afraid of the conclusions I might be forced to draw.

Maybe I should have told my parents in the first place about what happened on Saturday night.

Maybe I should tell them as soon as I get home after the show. I'll just say—

Suddenly, one of the characters on stage utters something that lurches me right out of my reverie.

I snap to attention and listen frantically to the dialogue.

Riley, noticing that I've suddenly stiffened in my seat, leans over and whispers, "Is everything all right?"

"What did that girl just call that guy?"

"Which girl?"

"The one in the white bonnet," I whisper urgently. "She just said his name, didn't she?"

Someone in the row behind us hisses, "Shhh!"

"Sorry," Riley says over his shoulder, then leans into my ear and says in the barest whisper, "It was Zachariah Wellbourne."

The words slam into me like a two-by-four, and I can't seem to find my breath.

I gape at the stage, where the female character in a drab gray dress and white apron is flirting with the male character. He's wearing a style that's now familiar to me—dark breeches and a matching jacket, a white blouse with a pointy, wide collar that spreads out over his shoulders, and a broad-brimmed hat.

And his name is Zachariah Wellbourne.

Oh my God.

As soon as I heard it, I recognized it.

The boy who broke into our house—the boy with the old-fashioned clothing and the British accent—the boy who thinks it's still 1693—was named Zachariah Wellbourne.

Riley doesn't seem to notice that I'm not breathing. He's just watching the action on stage, like everyone else in the audience.

And I'm sitting here with panic threatening to choke me.

But I have to pay attention. I have to find out what's going on.

I force myself to calm down and listen to the actors. It's not easy to hear them over the uproar inside my head. This frantic inner voice keeps screaming at me that something very peculiar—and maybe even dangerous—is definitely going on.

But I have to concentrate if I'm going to figure out what it is.

I frown, trying to decipher the conversation between the two actors on stage. Where's that boring narrator when I need him?

But after a few minutes, I start to get the gist of the scene. The redheaded girl in the white bonnet is supposed to be Felicity Crane. The guy, Zachariah Wellbourne, is her father's new young apprentice. Obviously, these two are flirting outrageously with each other.

Then another character comes onstage—a heavyset black woman wearing a turban. I know before they confirm it that she's Jemima, the slave. She tells Felicity that her parents are looking for her, and the scene ends.

You can hear the crew moving furniture around behind the curtain, setting up for the next scene.

Riley shifts in his seat and casually drops his arm across the back of my chair. I barely notice. My thoughts are tumbling over each other and my hands are shaking so badly that I clutch the armrests just to keep them steady. I'm battling the overwhelming urge to escape—to jump up and run out of here. But I can't. I have to find out what's going on, and this stupid play might tell me.

The curtain rises again after a moment, and the stage is set up to look like the inside of someone's house. There's a big cardboard fireplace and fake windows with curtains along the back wall. The furniture is real, though—spindle-backed chairs and a few tables and a spinning wheel.

The stage is dark. Felicity and Jemima sneak into the room carrying candles. The slave starts telling Felicity about witchcraft, and how she can cast spells on people and put hexes on them. Then Felicity's father, Josiah Crane, shows up and hollers at both of them.

In the next scene, Zachariah and Felicity are supposed to be outside. They stand under a big cardboard tree that looks dangerously tilted, talking about how no one has seen Jemima in days.

Riley leans over and whispers in my ear, "Yeah, that's 'cause the old man got rid of her, like this," and he slashes a finger across his throat.

"Shh . . ." I'm trying to hear what Zachariah and Felicity are saying to each other.

It's something about how they're falling in love, and before you know it, they're kissing passionately. If you ask me, the actress is really into it, not wanting to come up for air, but the actor who's playing Zachariah kind of looks like he's trying to get out of her clutches.

Riley's arm drops from the back of my chair to rest against my shoulders. I'm wearing my sleeveless black dress, and his fingers make contact with the bare skin of my upper arm. His touch sends a little thrill careening through me, and I'm momentarily distracted from my mission.

Then I get a grip. *You need to concentrate on this pageant, not on Riley Kennedy,* I scold myself. But it isn't easy. I twist slightly in my seat so that his fingers aren't against my skin. He gets the message and shifts position, moving his arm away.

Despite my relief, I feel a twinge of regret. He probably thinks I'm trying to tell him I'm not that kind of girl. I wish I could explain that under normal circumstances, I would gladly be that kind of girl, but right now, I'm on a mission and he's too distracting.

The curtain falls as Felicity and Zachariah are kissing. The narrator steps into a spotlight and begins speaking.

"The future looks rosy for these young lovers, but alas, 'twas not meant to be." He delivers this information in a total deadpan. "Unrest is looming on the horizon. 'Tis the spring of 1692, and in nearby Salem, a group of young girls is pinpointing witches from among the most upstanding citizens in the community. Seacliffe is filled with news of the infamous witchcraft trials. And before long, the frenzied madness spreads throughout the Massachusetts Bay."

The curtain rises again and the scene has shifted to the town square. A young woman, whose name turns out to be Elspeth Andrewes, is convincing some men that she saw Felicity Crane "bewitching" Zachariah Wellbourne. They believe her, because apparently, Zachariah hasn't been seen for days, just like Jemima. The men arrest Felicity under suspicion of witchcraft.

The next thing you know, everyone is in a courthouse and people are testifying against Felicity. As evidence of her guilt, they cite ridiculous examples of how she's bewitched them. One woman says that Felicity walked by her window as she was sitting there, spinning, and a moment later, her spinning wheel broke. And a man says that Felicity's red hair is evidence of the "devil's flame," whatever that means.

Each of these pieces of evidence brings solemn nods from the people seated on benches in the courtroom.

The actress playing Felicity keeps weeping and moaning and swaying like she's about to keel over, and she's so irritating that I find myself wishing they'd shoot her on the spot.

Finally, after everyone else has had their say, Elspeth stands up and pleads with the court to stop Felicity, "before she makes the rest of us disappear one by one."

The scene ends with the magistrate saying, "Felicity Crane, you are hereby found guilty of practicing witchcraft. As punishment, you will be hanged and die."

I'm horrified by the harsh words, despite the melodramatic shrieks of the actress playing Felicity.

I look at Riley. Even he seems a little affected by it.

The curtain falls and the narrator steps forward once again. In a monotonous tone, he says, "Shortly after Felicity Crane was convicted, Elspeth Andrewes, the girl who had accused her, mysteriously vanished. Felicity Crane was executed by the terrified and vengeant people of Seacliffe on the twenty-first of June, 1693."

I gulp and glance over at Riley.

He whispers, "Seen her ghost yet?"

I scowl at him and focus back on the narrator.

"Just before the execution," he drones, "an unfamiliar young woman appeared in Seacliffe. She was dressed in strange, exotic robes and adorned with magic charms. The people of Seacliffe were taking no chances. The stranger, too, was accused of witchcraft and was swiftly brought to trial. Within twenty-four hours of Felicity Crane's execution, the second young woman had been convicted of witchcraft."

He pauses and adjusts his fake wire-rimmed glasses. Just when I think he's finished speaking and the show is over, he starts up again.

"But that very night, a fierce storm blew in from the sea. It destroyed houses, and several people were killed by the violent winds. The townspeople feared that the tempest had been sent by the evil spirit of Felicity Crane. As soon as it passed, the stranger was hung. To this day, her identity has remained a mystery. No one ever knew her name, or where she was from, but that didn't matter to the people of Seacliffe. The madness was over."

This is crazy. I *know* it's crazy, and yet, I can't help it. I have to go through with it.

I've been telling myself that for hours now, as the plan formed in my mind.

I first thought of it as Riley was driving me out along Route 1A, heading toward Eddie's drive-in restaurant. I was staring out the window at the woods that line the highway, and it came to me.

Riley didn't seem to notice how distracted I was. And as soon as we got to the drive-in, he spotted some of his friends.

"Mind if they join us?" he asked me as they approached our table.

"Of course not," I said. I was relieved to have the burden of making conversation lifted.

I know Riley's friends—two guys, Shawn and Rich, and their dates, Cindy and Deborah Jo—probably thought I was a bore. All I did was go through the motions. I was too busy plotting.

The only time I came halfway out of my trance was when Riley walked me to the back door at the end of the night. I was prepared to strong-arm him and deliver my usual spiel about how I'm not the kind of girl who kisses on the first date. But he didn't try anything, just gave my arm a little squeeze and said, "See you."

In passing, I wondered if he hadn't tried anything because he's a gentleman, or if he's concluded I'm a wet blanket and he has no desire to kiss me.

But that speculation was quickly nudged right out of my brain as I briefly greeted my parents, who were watching television in the keeping room, and headed upstairs.

Now it's way past midnight, and they're both in bed. The house is quiet. And it's time.

I slip, fully dressed, out of my room and down the hall. At the top of the stairs, I pause and listen to make sure no one is stirring. My father's snoring is still rhythmic, reverberating from beneath their closed bedroom door.

Swiftly, I tiptoe down the steps and through the house. If I allow myself the slightest hesitation, I know I'm going to back out and hightail it back to my bed.

In the kitchen, I take a sharp paring knife from the block on the counter. I don't know if I'd ever actually bring myself to use it as a weapon, but I have to know I have the option. I slip it carefully into my pocket.

In the broom closet next to the entryway is my father's emergency flashlight. I take it out and turn it on to make sure the batteries are working. The beam of light seems reassuringly bright.

It's now or never.

Clutching the flashlight in one trembling hand, I use the other to slide the bolt from the back door. It creaks as I push it open, sounding ear-shattering in the silence. I freeze, my hand still on the knob, waiting for footsteps above and my father's voice calling out, "Who's down there?"

But all I hear is my own heart pounding in my ears, and the crickets chirping away outside.

After a moment, I take a deep breath and slip out into the night.

The air is warm and there's no breeze. It's not hard to find my way across the yard in the moonlight, but things grow shadowy when I reach the line of trees at the back.

I turn on the flashlight, aiming it toward the path between the trees. Out here in the open, the beam of yellow light seems feeble and pale.

You're crazy. Go back.

But the frightened little voice inside my head doesn't have any effect.

As if propelled by some unseen automatic force, I keep going. I hold the flashlight in my right hand as I pick my way along the path through the woods. In my left hand, I'm clutching the knife handle inside my pocket.

The water can't be too far away—I can hear the pounding waves and smell the salty sea scent. And the woods aren't actually woods at all. After I get through those first few trees at the back of our property, things open up and before long, the path is winding among soft sand dunes. The only vege-tation is some low scrub brush and some long sea grass.

There's a breeze now, gently blowing off the water.

I continue walking, taking deep breaths to calm myself.

And suddenly, I realize that the smell of the ocean is min-gling with something else.

What is it?

I stand still and sniff.

Wood smoke.

An instant after I identify the scent, I see a flicker ahead.

Someone has built a fire out here in the dunes.

Peering into the shadows, I can just make out an orange glow close to the ground.

I gingerly move forward, relieved that I can't even hear my own footsteps—they're completely drowned out by the pounding surf nearby.

A few more steps and I should be able to see . . .

There.

I stop and take it all in.

The little fire in the sand, bordered by a careful ring of stones.

The crude spit stretching over the flames, upon which something—a small animal—is impaled.

And the dark figure crouched before the fire.

Zachariah Wellbourne.

TEN

As though he senses that he's being watched, he looks up, startled.

Instantly, he jumps to his feet. Despite his tall figure looming just a few feet away, I feel my own terror dribbling away. It's evident in the way he's staring at me—or rather, at the beam from my flashlight, which is aimed directly at him—that he's petrified.

Squinting into the glare, he moves his hands up in front of him in a protective gesture, as if fending me off.

Boldly, I take a step closer, half expecting him to bolt. But he doesn't move. He seems frozen in fear.

"I want to talk to you," I say, walking toward him.

He flinches, but still doesn't look up at my face. He's riveted by the flashlight, as though he's never seen one before.

Maybe he hasn't, a little voice whispers inside my mind, and a sudden chill shoots over my body.

"Are you Zachariah Wellbourne?" I ask, stopping in front of him.

He nods.

"How old are you?" I ask, because it's the only thing I can think of. My thoughts are careening as wildly as the bumper cars at Palisades Park. I've got to get ahold of myself, think rationally.

There's a long pause.

"How old?" I repeat, struggling to maintain control.

"S-seventeen years," he stammers at last, in that weird accent.

"When were you born?"

He swallows hard. "In March."

"What year?" I move the flashlight for emphasis, and he throws a hand up against his face. I see that he's trembling all over, but I can't let myself feel sorry for him. I *can't.* "Answer me!"

"Sixteen hundred and seventy-five," he says in a choked voice, and for the first time, our eyes collide.

Sixteen seventy-five.

"Please—do not hurt me . . ."

I can't respond.

I can't think.

I can't breathe.

"Please," he says again.

I'm staring blankly into his pleading gaze, unable to grasp anything he's saying.

Gradually, though, as he makes another plea, my head clears. Some instinct takes over—an abrupt determination to remain levelheaded and logical in the face of the impossible claim he's making.

"You're insane," I tell him calmly. "You can't have been born in sixteen seventy-five. That was over three hundred years ago. And your name can't be Zachariah Wellbourne."

He looks me in the eye, and suddenly I see a spark of anger in those large brown eyes of his. " 'Tis Zachariah Wellbourne," he says almost defiantly. His spine seems a little straighter now, and he's lowered his hands slightly.

"It is not." I shake my head in denial.

" 'Tis."

I start to say " 'tisn't," then realize that this is crazy.

"Look," I go, starting again, "Be reasonable. You've played your little game long enough. Now what's your name? I mean your real name?"

"I might ask thee the same question."

"Fair enough. I'm Abbey—Abigail—Harmon."

"Abigail."

"Right. And you are . . . ?"

He lifts his chin. "Zachariah Wellbourne."

"All right, Zachariah Wellbourne," I say, trying to keep my voice level, "if you were born that long ago, how can you be only seventeen years old? *I'm* almost seventeen years old, and I was born in 1946."

He just shrugs.

"Well?" I'm losing my patience. "Answer me!"

"I do not know."

"You *do* know," I say through clenched teeth, "that the year is 1963?"

For a moment, we just stare at each other. Then, in a voice so quiet I can barely hear him, he says, "Yes."

"Now we're getting somewhere. If this is 1963, then what are you doing here? You can't have just been hanging around for three hundred years. I mean, what the heck did you do, discover the fountain of youth?" I try to laugh, but the sound that comes out is hollow and strangled.

He's just studying me, and I can't read the expression on his face. I clear my throat. "Let's try again. Just how did you get here from the sixteen hundreds?"

He doesn't answer me.

"I said, how did you get here?"

He's silent.

I try a different tactic. "Are you a ghost?"

"No!" he says immediately. If I'm not mistaken, he looks insulted.

"Fine," I tell him. "So you're not a ghost. What are you?"

When he still doesn't reply, I find myself starting to get angry. "Look," I say evenly, "if you don't start talking and tell me who you are and what you're doing here and why you've been lurking around my house, I'm going to use this on you." To punctuate my threat, I gesture with the flashlight, and he cringes away from the beam.

Finally he speaks. "That object in thy hand . . . 'tis a weapon?"

"You'd better believe 'tis a weapon, Buster. All I have to do is press a button, and this thing will send out a bolt of lightning that will strike you dead."

"No!" He recoils in horror, and I feel a twinge of guilt.

But then I remember how he's been terrorizing me ever since I got to Seacliffe. So I just shrug and go, "Well, then, you'd better start talking, hadn't you?"

I can see that he's so terrified of me and my "weapon" that he can't seem to find his voice.

To nudge him, I say, "You know Felicity Crane, don't you?"

At the mere mention of her name, he snaps into action. "Felicity Crane . . . yes . . . how dost thee know that name?"

Somehow, I don't think this is the time to bring up the fact that she's famous—or infamous—as the first witch to be executed in Seacliffe.

"Tell me who she is," I command instead.

And despite his fear, his voice softens as he speaks of her. "Felicity is my beloved . . . she is good and kind and gentle."

I'm not sure what to say to that. I just nod.

He narrows his eyes at me. "Thou hast seen Felicity?"

Immediately, I shake my head.

"Yet thou speaketh of her."

"I've heard of her, that's all," I say defensively, irritated by the suspicion in his gaze.

And anyway, how did he get control of this conversation? "Now tell me why you have been lurking around my house," I say sternly.

He hesitates.

I brandish the flashlight just to show him who's still boss.

Immediately he launches into nervous conversation. Because of his accent, I can barely understand him, but he says something like, "I mean thee no harm. I only want to enter thy dwelling."

"Why?"

"I cannot say."

"You'd *better* say if you want to stay alive," I inform him in my best gangster imitation.

He casts his eyes at the ground. And then he begins speaking in a voice so low I can barely hear him. I step closer.

The first word I can make out is "witchcraft."

". . . and she learned it from Jemima, the Negro woman who came to Seacliffe from an exotic island. Felicity—"

"Speak up and slow down, please. You're telling me Felicity practiced witchcraft?" I interrupt, just to make sure I heard him correctly.

"Yes," he says in a whisper. "But 'twas not the work of the devil. My beloved Felicity harmed no one. She assured me that with the magical powers, she could do good, could heal illness and troubles."

"How? By casting spells?"

"Yes. And with charms that Jemima gave her. And herbs."

"Herbs?"

"Yes. I once saw her heal a sheep by rubbing an herbal balm on its injured leg."

"Besides healing, what else could she do with these powers?"

He stares at me, as if he's unwilling to say.

My heart is pounding. "Tell me."

"She could travel . . ."

"Travel where?"

He looks me in the eye and says flatly, "Through time."

With piercing clarity, the pieces of the puzzle slam into place in my brain. And somehow, as preposterous as the explanation is, I'm relieved to acknowledge it at last.

"You came here from the past," I say quietly. "Felicity sent you here."

He nods.

I take a deep breath, then let it out slowly, looking at the dark starry sky. "Oh my God. It can't be."

For a long time, I can't muster my voice.

Finally, I look back at him and manage one word. "How?"

"Jemima taught her. She drew a magical pentagram on the dirt floor of the secret cupboard. And then—"

"Secret cupboard? Where?"

" 'Tis in the keeping room. Beside the fireplace."

But I knew which cupboard he meant before he said it. It's still there—a cramped, narrow space beside the chimney—and it's actually more of a closet.

According to that book Katie brought over yesterday, Jemima's ghost had been seen near the fireplace in the keeping room. But what if it wasn't her ghost after all . . . ?

"But," I say, frowning, "that cupboard isn't secret. Anyone can see it."

He nods. "Inside the closet beside the fireplace, along the back wall, a secret door is concealed. There is a small lever hidden in the ceiling of the closet, and when pressed lightly, the door springs open. A similar lever above the door inside the secret cupboard opens it for anyone who is hiding inside."

"But who would be hiding inside?"

He just shrugs.

I guess when people built houses in the olden days, they liked to think of everything.

"After drawing the pentagram on the floor of the secret cupboard," Zachariah continues, "Jemima cast a spell using an incantation that she would not reveal, not even to Felicity. But the pentagram was bewitched ever afterward."

I just stare at him. He doesn't see me. He's looking into the crackling fire as he speaks, as though he's recollecting the details more for his own benefit than for mine.

"One night, Jemima brought Felicity to the cupboard. She showed her herbs that had been hanging from the rafters at the back of the closet to dry. 'Twas an exotic, foreign herb she had brought with her from the island and planted in the soil beside the house. She told Felicity she had not expected the herb to survive the change in climate."

"But it did?"

"Yes. And she sprinkled the dried leaves of the herb into the center of the pentagram. Then she stood on that spot, closed her eyes, and closed the door. Felicity could hear her repeating the year she wished to visit—1792, one hundred years in the future. Before Felicity knew it, there was silence behind the door. She opened it and Jemima was gone."

That's it. This is too much.

"Wait a minute—this is ridiculous," I say, holding up a hand. "You're telling me that the keeping room cupboard is some kind of time travel booth, and I'm sitting here believing you. What's wrong with me?"

" 'Tis true," he protests earnestly.

"Oh, yeah? How do you know?" But even as I say it, I realize what his answer will be. He's here in 1963, isn't he?

But I don't really believe that he's from the past.

Do I?

Of course you don't.

He could have made the whole time travel story up.

Of course he did. He's just some crackpot local who's been pushed over the edge by this town's obsession with the past.

But what about the stories about Jemima's "ghost" always being seen near the fireplace in the keeping room?

What about them? What do they prove?

I look over at him and see that he's staring off into space. I'm about to tell him what I think of his idiotic story when he begins speaking again, in a faraway voice.

"Jemima never came back. Felicity didn't tell a soul what she knew. Then the townspeople began whispering that Felicity's father, Josiah Crane, had killed Jemima."

I find myself nodding, remembering the rumor's role in local legend.

"Fearing that her father would be accused of murder, Felicity turned to me in desperation. She shared the story of Jemima's disappearance, and I did not believe her. She told me that she would prove it to me, and that she intended to then prove it to the townspeople so that her father's good name might be cleared."

Despite my doubts, I'm hanging on his every word as though he's telling the truth.

"I agreed to meet her in the keeping room at midnight, after her family was asleep. And there, inside the cupboard, she showed me the magic pentagram traced into the dirt and the dried herbs in the rafters. She pinched off some of the leaves, crumbled them between her fingers, and sprinkled the dust into the center of the pentagram.

"She told me that she would like to take me one year into the future, to 1693. She had traveled there herself only the night before—the fourteenth of June."

I make a snorting noise and dismiss him with a wave of my hand. "How did she know she was in the future?"

"I made the same inquiry," he informs me. "As she was in the closet repeating the year and concentrating, she felt a sudden, curious tingling over her entire body. Startled, she opened the closet door and found that the keeping room looked much the same. But when she crept through the house, she discovered a letter Goodwife Crane was writing to her sister in England. It told of Felicity's marriage to me"—at this he smiles slightly—"which had taken place just after the new year. The ink was still wet, and the letter bore the same date—the fourteenth of June—in the year 1693."

I'm shaking my head. "That doesn't mean anything," I tell Zachariah firmly, shoving away the thought that maybe I'm the one I'm trying to convince. "And if she really was in the future, how did she come back?"

"The herbs were still tucked away in the top of the closet. She sprinkled them into the pentagram, which was still barely visible on the floor, and uttered the words, '1692.' " He looks at me as if that's all the explanation I need.

"You expect me to believe that?"

He gives me a rueful little smile. "I, too, had doubt when Felicity told me her preposterous story. 'Twas why she insisted upon showing me. And when I met her in the keeping room that evening, she asked me to stand in the middle of the pentagram with her. We began concentrating, repeating '1693' over and over again."

"What happened?"

"Nothing." Before I can respond, he goes on, looking a little embarrassed, "Felicity thought that perhaps standing so close to her was causing me to—well, I could not concentrate. She instructed me to remain in the closet. She stepped out, closed the door, and told me to concentrate and continue to repeat the year. I did. And then I felt a peculiar sensation pass over my body."

My jaw is hanging open now. I have to lean closer to hear him, because his head is bent and he's staring at the ground as he speaks in a near whisper.

"When I opened the door, Felicity was gone. The room looked different. There were strange things . . . contraptions I had never before seen. Yet the rooms were familiar and appeared to be in the same dwelling. I walked through the house looking for Felicity, expecting to find her hiding upstairs in her bedchamber. But when I reached the top of the stairs, I found . . ."

His voice trails off.

"What?" I ask him in a hushed tone. "What did you find?"

He lifts his head and looks directly into my eyes. "I found a stranger . . . I found thee, Abigail."

ELEVEN

I don't know at which point I turned the flashlight off, put it down, and sat beside Zachariah on a log near the fire. And I don't know when I started believing his bizarre story.

Maybe it was when he was telling me how desperate he is to get back to 1693, where he thinks Felicity must be worried about him. He sounded so desperate, so earnest, that I had to take him seriously.

He's wondering why Felicity didn't follow him into the future, as she was supposed to. When I suggested that maybe she thought he was in 1693, he shook his head. "She must have heard me say 1963," he insisted. "I must return to her, for something may be wrong."

I don't have the heart to tell him that back in 1692, right about now, his beloved is probably sitting in jail, accused of witchcraft and awaiting execution.

Or maybe I started believing him when he was describing how he's been hiding here along the water for the past few days, keeping an eye on our house so that, as soon as it looked deserted, he can sneak inside to the cupboard. I mean, I know that's true. I caught him doing it.

Anyway, we both let down our guards and somehow, now he doesn't seem very mysterious—or even nutty—at all. And I don't think he's quite as scared of me, now, either. He seems glad to have someone to talk to.

"Willst thou help me get back, Abigail?" he asks finally, as we both stare into the crackling flames.

I'm still so dazed that it takes a moment for me to respond. "Help you get back? Uh, sure. All you need to do is go into the cupboard and say 1693, right?"

He shakes his head and his shaggy black hair brushes back and forth along the wide white collar spread across his shoulders. "No. I must have the dried herbs, as well."

"Where are they?"

He looks bleak. "I had hoped they would still be growing along the back wall of thy dwelling."

I give him a dubious look. "After almost three hundred years?"

" 'Twas meant to be only one year. In my haste to repeat the year 1693, I must have interchanged the two middle digits. 'Tis how I came to be here in 1963."

"I know, I know." He already explained that part. I can't help shaking my head.

I guess I have a hard time seeing how repeating "1693" over and over again is such a tongue twister. Okay, maybe if you're nervous enough—and standing alone in a dark closet—you could get it confused, but still . . .

"And I had taken a sprig of the dried herbs with me," he's saying, "clutched in my hand, so that I would have them if I needed them, but—"

"I know, I know, you dropped them when you were trying to escape from me—and no, I didn't find them inside the house," I add, sensing that he's about to ask me that question for the millionth time. "If you did drop them inside the house, they're long gone. My parents would have thrown away a dried bunch of leaves and stems if they found them on the floor."

He looks so dejected that I say hopefully, "Maybe you'll

remember what the herb was so that we can find some some-where else. You know, at a greenhouse or something."

"Greenhouse?" He looks puzzled.

"A place where exotic plants and herbs are grown. If you just knew what it was called . . ."

He shakes his shaggy head ruefully. "No. I never knew the name of the plant. Felicity told me not."

"But you know what it looks like."

"Yes. And it has a pungent, distinctive odor."

"Well, what are we waiting for? Let's go see if we can find it in the shrubs around the house. My mother keeps saying that whole area needs to be weeded out, but she hasn't done it yet."

I stand up and brush off the back of my black capri pants—which he's been eyeing uncomfortably. I guess he's used to women wearing those high-collared, long, full-skirted dresses all the time, with bonnets on their heads.

He stands, too, then casts a wary look at the flashlight, which is still on the ground. I bend over, scoop it up, and flick it on. Instantly, he jumps back, away from it.

"Zachariah?"

"Yes?" he asks, cowering.

"This isn't a weapon." When he looks at me blankly, I try it his way. " 'Tis not a weapon."

He raises his brows.

"I only said that so you would be afraid of me," I admit. "I'm sorry."

He nods, but doesn't look like he believes me. He keeps staring at the beam of light.

Finally, he goes, " 'Tis some kind of lantern, is it not?"

"Yes. That's right." And that's when it dawns on me that he would be astonished if he could grasp the scope of how different life in 1963 must be from the way things were back in his era.

I mean, what would he think of cars? Or airplanes? Or how about refrigerators, hi-fis, washing machines, and television sets?

And what if I told him that right now, while we're standing here, two Russian astronauts, Valery Bykovsky and Valentina Tereshkova, are miles above us, orbiting in space? Or that President Kennedy promises that we'll be landing a man on the moon someday in the near future?

A man on the moon!

I mean, I don't even know if *I* can comprehend that.

I look at Zachariah. He's carefully spreading sand over the fire to douse the flames, keeping one skeptical eye on me and the flashlight. It sure would be fun to introduce him to the modern world.

But then I realize that, considering how terrified he was of a mere flashlight, he would probably have a heart attack if he saw an airplane or even a television set. And I can't help feeling a little protective of him.

So when he finishes putting out the fire and looks at me, I can't help patting his arm and saying, "Don't worry, Zachariah. We'll get you back there somehow."

He doesn't look entirely convinced, and I'm not about to tell him that I'm not, either.

"I miss my dear Felicity," is all he says.

"I'll bet." I turn away from him. I don't want my face to give anything away. What's going to happen when he gets back and finds out his dear Felicity is about to be—or already has been—sentenced to death? He's going to be—

Wait a minute.

I just remembered something.

According to that play tonight, none of the people who disappeared from Seacliffe were ever heard from again.

Including Zachariah.

So unless the historians in this town are wrong, he's not going to be able to get back there. He might be stuck here in 1963 forever.

"Shall we depart, then?" he asks, behind me.

"Oh—yeah." I keep my back to him. I'm afraid my expression might give away the truth—that unless history can be rewritten, he's not going anywhere.

We walk silently and single-file back along the path, following the flashlight's beam. When we reach the edge of the woods, I pause and say, "Wait one second." I just want to make sure our house is still dark and quiet. It must be three or four in the morning by this time—the sky is even starting to look a little lighter.

I peer through the bordering fringe of trees, across the yard, to where the big, boxy lines of the house loom against the sky. All the windows are still dark, which is a good sign.

I turn back to Zachariah. "All right. It looks like everyone is still asleep. Let's go."

We hurry across the yard to the back of the house. I look expectantly at Zachariah. "Well? Where were the herbs?"

He points vaguely to the tangle of shrubs and weeds that line the foundation. "There."

"I'll hold the flashlight and you crawl in there and look." *I'm* certainly not about to get down on my hands and knees in that jungle. What if there are snakes or bugs in there?

Zachariah looks agreeable and immediately drops to the ground. I try to use the flashlight beam to illuminate the undergrowth so that he can see what he's doing.

I can hear him sniffing around and muttering to himself. "Hey, try to be a little more quiet, will you?" I whisper to him. "My parents' bedroom window is right up there, and it's open."

Just as I finish saying that, he shouts out, "Yes! 'Tis here!"

His voice shatters the peaceful night, and almost instantly, a light goes on in the second story window above our heads.

"It's my parents!" I hiss. "Stay down!" I leap into the bushes and flatten myself against the wall of the house.

Through the open window, I can hear my father's voice, and then my mother's. They must be standing right in the window looking out, because I can hear every word they're saying.

"It doesn't look like there's anyone down there." That's my father, sounding sleepy.

"Frank, how can you be so lazy after what happened this afternoon? Go down there and make sure! I'll check on the kids."

I hear him grumbling and moving away from the window.

"Whatever you do," I whisper frantically to Zachariah, "stay down in these bushes. Don't you dare move!"

My mind is spinning. I have to give myself up. I don't have a choice, because my mother is about to discover I'm not in my bed.

Before my father can mistake me for a prowler and hit me over the head with something hard, I boldly walk up the back steps and open the back door. Just to make sure he hears me and doesn't think I'm someone who's trying to sneak in, I start whistling a jaunty version of "Love Me Do."

"Who's there? Abigail, is that you?" He's standing in the kitchen in his pajamas, holding his old wooden bat like a weapon. What did I tell you?

"Yeah. Oh, hi, Dad!" I try to sound casual. "What are you doing up?"

"What am *I* doing up? Abigail, do you know what time it is?"

"Uh . . . early?"

"Late! Too late for you to be sneaking out of this house."

"Dad, I didn't sneak out. I got up early so that I could . . . take a walk."

Oh, sure. That's so lame, even *I* wouldn't believe me.

He doesn't. "Abigail Elizabeth Harmon, you are in big trouble."

"For going for a walk?"

"Since when do you get up at three in the morning?"

"Since we moved here. The stupid sun rises in the middle of the night," I point out truthfully.

"Well, it's not up now. And I find it hard to believe someone who can never make it to school on time at eight o'clock when she says she got up at three A.M. to take a walk."

It's true. I am a late sleeper. But what am I supposed to tell him?

It gets worse.

"And you're wearing the same thing you had on when you got home from your date," he goes on, gesturing at my black capri pants and sleeveless black top. "And you have makeup on, too. I wasn't born yesterday, Abigail."

"Frank? Is that Abbey?" I hear my mother's footsteps on the stairs. "What happened?"

"Go back to bed, Grace. She's fine. Nothing happened."

"Are you sure?"

"I'm sure."

"Abbey?"

"I'm fine, Mom," I call out.

"Good," she says around a yawn, and goes back upstairs.

My father and I look at each other again. Boy, does he look angry.

"All right, then, Dad—what do *you* think I'm doing?" Might as well let him tell me. *I* can't think of a single reason I'd be out in the middle of the night dressed like this.

He sets his mouth grimly. "I think you're sneaking out with that Kennedy boy."

"Riley?" This explanation catches me so off guard that all I can do is stare at my dad.

"That's right."

"You think I was sneaking out to meet Riley."

"Yes. I do."

I hate to do this, but I have no choice. I drop my gaze to the floor and say, "Well, I guess you caught me."

A flash of disappointment crosses his face before anger sets in. "I guess so."

"What are you going to do about this?" I ask meekly, feeling guilty. If only I could tell him the truth! But some instinct warns me that I can't do that to Zachariah. I can't get anyone else involved.

"I'll have to think about your punishment. Right now, I'll tell you what *you're* going to do. You're going to march right upstairs to your room and climb into your bed and stay there until the morning."

I shrug. "Fine."

And then I walk out of the kitchen, probably leaving him wondering why I'm not giving him an argument, which I would usually do under these circumstances.

When I get upstairs, I shut my door and hurry over to my window. I can't see Zachariah hiding in the bushes, but I sense that he's still there. I know I can't risk calling down to him. I hope he'll know enough not to move or make any noise.

After a few minutes, I hear my father coming back upstairs and going into his room across the hall.

And after about ten more minutes, he's snoring steadily again.

I put my face against the window screen and whisper, "Zachariah? If you're there, don't answer me. Just listen. Wait a few more minutes. Then get out of here. I'll come and find you tomorrow by the water, where we met tonight."

I listen intently and think I hear a quiet rustling in the bushes.

"Good night," I call softly into the darkness. Then I tiptoe across the room and climb into bed.

Poor Zachariah. This whole thing is useless. Even if he manages to find the herbs, he's obviously not going to be able to go anywhere. History can't be rewritten . . .

Suddenly, my eyelids, which were starting to droop, snap open again.

Who says we can't change history?

Zachariah said Felicity already went from 1692 to 1693 and back again.

If she managed to travel backward, she could have gone even further back—say, fifty years—and done something that would have changed the course of history.

Like, what if she knew from some lesson in school that a major Indian massacre on the settlers had taken place on a certain date in history? She could have traveled back in time, shown up at the settlement and warned the people there of impending attack so they could escape!

And if that could happen, what if Zachariah can go back to 1692 now and *save* Felicity somehow? Would history books be instantly altered? Would the monument to Seacliffe's executed teenaged witch suddenly vanish—because she wasn't put to death after all?

Suddenly, my head is filled with possibilities and puzzles.

I'm completely confused and overwhelmed by the implications of this new idea.

Stifling a yawn, I roll over onto my stomach and try to clear my head.

All at once I'm exhausted, mentally and physically.

All I want to do is stop thinking about what happened tonight, what's going to happen tomorrow—and what might still happen three hundred years ago—and go to sleep.

So I do.

TWELVE

When I first wake up on Wednesday morning, I lie there with my eyes closed, thinking that there's something I'm supposed to remember—something that happened last night.

Then it all comes back to me in a rush, and I wince.

Oh, yeah.

The pageant. Riley. Zachariah. The herbs. Getting caught. My father.

I don't want to face this day.

I lie there for a few more minutes, then decide I might as well get it over with.

I take my time washing up and getting dressed in dark green Bermuda shorts and a mustard-colored top. I strap my watch on, noting that it's almost ten o'clock.

Then I comb out my hair, tease and spray it, and put on a dark green headband.

I polish the silver Beatles medallion that's hanging, as always, around my neck. I do an especially good job on Ringo's miniature carved head, buffing it until it shines.

I painstakingly apply makeup.

I make my bed.

I straighten up the room.

Finally, I can't stall any longer.

I head downstairs, trying to look on the bright side.

After all, you never know. Maybe my parents will have

forgotten about what happened. My father might think it was just a nightmare.

Oh, sure.

Well, then, maybe they'll just write it off as a silly teenage prank. Maybe they'll even tell me amusing stories about similar things they pulled when they were my age.

But somehow, I can't picture my mother ever sneaking out in the middle of the night to meet some boy. Or if she did, she certainly wouldn't admit it.

So that's out.

But maybe no one is home and I won't have to deal with anything.

No such luck.

Both of my parents are in the kitchen, drinking coffee and talking in low voices.

As soon as I reluctantly walk in, they stop and look up. They don't look thrilled to see me.

"Hi, Mom! Hi, Dad!" I try to sound sunny and casual.

"Sit down, Abigail," is all my father says.

Uh-oh.

He only calls me by my full name when he's really, really steamed about something.

I pull out a chair and plop glumly into it.

"Your mother and I have discussed your actions last night."

I'll just bet they have.

"First of all, we want you to know how disappointed we are. We didn't think that we had raised the kind of daughter who would sneak out in the middle of the night to meet a boy."

Oh, geez. I can't believe this is happening.

I wish I could blurt out the whole truth, but I have to

protect Zachariah. All I can do is sit there silently and stare at my hands in my lap.

"Do you know what I thought when I heard someone sneaking around last night?" my father continues. "After what Joe said yesterday about someone trying to break into the house, I thought you were a prowler. It's a darn good thing I realized it was you, Abigail, because I was all set to use that bat."

"Abbey, what were you thinking?" my mother puts in. "This isn't the kind of behavior that a young lady—"

"Grace," my father interrupts, "I'll handle this. Abigail, we thought you were trustworthy, but apparently you aren't. As a result, we're going to have to take away your privileges so that we can keep an eye on you."

I open my mouth to protest, but he says, "I don't want to hear it. You let us down. Until we feel that we can trust you again, you're going to be grounded."

"Grounded!" I blurt out. "But that isn't fair."

"Fair? Young lady, what you did was not only irresponsible and underhanded, but it was dangerous. You're lucky I didn't hit you over the head with my bat, thinking you were that prowler."

"Oh, Frank."

"Grace, it could easily have happened."

"I know, but . . ." My mother shudders.

"So you're going to stay in this house all day and all night from now on, until we decide you've been punished long enough. Furthermore, there's a lot of work that needs to be done around here, and you're going to help us."

I just nod glumly.

Now what am I going to do?

I have to get to Zachariah somehow. I promised I'd meet him by the water today. He's going to wonder what happened to me. Besides, I have to help him get back to 1692 before it's too late.

Felicity was executed on June twenty-first—I remember that from the pageant. Normally I have a terrible time remembering names *and* dates, but since that's the longest day of the year—the solstice, as my mother called it—it stuck in my head.

According to what Zachariah said, the time travel only brings you to the exact same date in a different year. So if he were to travel back to 1692 today, it would be the nineteenth of June, two whole days before Felicity was murdered. He could somehow stop it from happening.

But that's not going to work unless I can get to him. And right now, it looks like I'm a prisoner in this house.

My father is out front with the workmen, still ripping away at the steps.

My mother is making me help her varnish the kitchen cupboards, which is disgusting, smelly work.

We've been at it for about two hours when my mother stretches, climbs off her chair, and says, "I've got to go get ready for my lunch date now. Oh, Abbey, can't you turn that thing down?"

One of my new favorite songs, "It's My Party," is blasting from my transistor radio on the counter. I reach over and adjust the volume. "You have a lunch date? With who?"

"Mary Kennedy," she says, going over to the sink and starting to scrub her hands. "We're going to the Lighthouse Inn up the highway."

Uh-oh.

"That's nice," I say, but all I can think is that if my mother mentions to Riley's mother that I was sneaking around with her son in the middle of the night, I'm in big trouble.

"After you finish that cupboard, you can stop for the day, Abbey," my mother says, drying her hands on a dish towel and surveying the cupboards. "It looks terrific."

"Mmm-hmm." I keep slapping varnish over the wood, trying to think of a way to stop her from going out to lunch.

The only thing I can think of is pretending to faint so that she'll get all worried and stay home to take care of me.

But before I can figure out how to go about it, she's on her way upstairs to get ready. Then I hear her call from the front hall, "Abbey?"

"What?"

"You got some mail here."

"I did?" I jump off the chair and hurry into the hall. My mother is looking at a white envelope.

"It looks like a letter from Brian," she says, giving me the eye. I know what she's thinking. That here he is, being sweet enough to write me a letter, and here I am, sneaking around in the night with another boy.

I should tell her the whole story.

Nah.

Why make things more complicated?

I just take the letter, mutter, "thanks," and scurry back into the kitchen.

I open the envelope and take out a single sheet of raggy notebook paper. There are exactly five lines on it, scrawled in dark and fairly illegible pencil and littered with misspellings—including my own name. Creep.

Dear Abby:

Hi. How are you? I am prety good. I miss you. How is everything in Seacliff? Everything here in New York

*is okay. I have been working a lot. Have you seen
"Cleoppattra" yet? I went with Louie and some of the
other fellas. It was dumb. Well, write back soon.*

Love,
Brian

I crumple the letter and toss it into the trash.

"Louie and the fellas—yeah, sure," I mutter under my
breath, climbing back onto the chair. I start savagely slapping
more varnish on the cupboards.

I'm so preoccupied with what a rat fink that Brian is that
I forget all about my mother's lunch date with Riley's mother
until I hear a knock on the door.

At the same exact moment, my mother comes back in, all
dressed up in her champagne-colored dress and hat and
gloves.

"Yoo hoo," Mrs. Kennedy calls through the screen.

"Oh, Mary, come on in. I just want to run out front and
tell Frank I'm leaving," my mother says before disappearing
toward the front of the house.

"And how are you, Abigail?" Mrs. Kennedy asks, stepping
into the kitchen. She's wearing a pink suit and pearls.

"I'm fine, thank you."

Maybe it's rude to keep working while she's here, but I
can't bring myself to stop and look at her. What if she says
something about—

"And did you enjoy the pageant last night, dear?"

Oh, great. I knew it.

"Yes," I say, swishing the paint brush around in the can
of varnish.

"Riley said he had a lovely time."

"That's nice."

My mother's heels are tapping back into the room. "All

set," she says, tucking her purse under her arm. "Abbey, I made tuna salad for you and Daddy and the workmen. There are rolls in the breadbox."

"Okay."

"After lunch, you can run the carpet sweeper in the front rooms."

"All right."

"And then dust all the furniture."

"Fine."

"I think that's it," my mother says, looking around. "Shall we go?" she asks Mrs. Kennedy.

"Yes. Good-bye, Abigail."

"Good-bye, Mrs. Kennedy. 'Bye, Mom."

They're gone.

And all I can do is hope for the best.

It's one-thirty and my mother still isn't back. My father and the two workmen, Joe and Clarence, have just finished the sandwiches I made and are outside again.

I can't believe how edgy I am. All I can think about is how Zachariah must be waiting for me down by the water. If only my father would leave for a little while, I could run down there and tell Zachariah what's going on.

But as it is, I'm helpless. There's no way I can get away.

Since I might as well get started on the chores my mother assigned, I go into the front hall and take the carpet sweeper out of the closet under the stairs.

I decide to start with the parlor, which is this small square room in the right front corner of the house. There's an ugly oriental area rug in there, and the carpet sweeper keeps getting caught up in all the fringe along the side.

By the time I'm finished with that room, I'm in a foul mood.

I'm in the front hall, grumbling and lugging the carpet sweeper to the foot of the steps, when I think I hear something.

Some sort of tapping noise.

At first, I think it's just my father and the workmen, who are right on the other side of the front door.

But I stand still and listen, and I hear it again.

It's not coming from outside.

It's definitely a tapping sound.

And it's coming from the keeping room.

My heart is thumping furiously as I creep over to the archway and peek around the corner into the room.

I don't know what I'm expecting to see.

But there's nothing there.

The room is quiet and undisturbed.

I scan the walls and furniture, just to make sure.

My eyes fall on the fireplace, and then on the narrow closet door beside it.

Suddenly remembering what Zachariah said about the secret cupboard inside, I decide to see if I can find it.

I walk over to the closet and yank the door open. The space inside is dark and cramped.

The right side of the closet is the redbrick chimney column. There are shelves built into the wall to my left, and they're cluttered with junk—old glass bottles and plates and cleaning supplies and stacks of magazines.

The back wall of the closet is made of rough-hewn wood, and it doesn't look like a door of any type.

Still, I'm determined to find the hidden latch. Zachariah said it was near the ceiling.

I step into the closet and glance overhead, but it's too dark to see anything.

What I need is a flashlight.

I go into the kitchen and reach for the one I used last night. Just before I grab it, I hear another noise in the keeping room. This time, it sounded like a voice.

A female voice.

And it was muffled.

I snatch the flashlight up and hurry back to the closet, then stand still in front of the open door, listening intently.

Nothing.

Was it my imagination?

I click on the flashlight and take a step forward, then stop dead.

I just heard it again.

It was definitely a female voice.

It was coming from behind the back wall of this closet.

And it clearly said, "1963."

Someone is inside the secret cupboard.

THIRTEEN

Frantically, before I can think twice about it, I shine the flashlight beam up into the dark corners above my head.

I scan the rough, aged wooden walls and ceilings, looking for something that might . . .

There!

Directly overhead.

Something that's about an inch square is protruding from the wall.

It looks like a tiny wooden bump . . . a lever?

Impulsively, I reach up and grab it, jiggling it with my fingers.

And suddenly, the entire back wall of the closet springs forward along one side.

Simultaneously, I hear a gasp from behind it, like someone was startled.

I slip my fingers around the edges of the secret door before she can pull it closed again.

"Felicity!" I hiss, "don't be afraid. I know all about everything. Zachariah is here. Come out and I'll take you to him."

As soon as I get those words out, the door is shoved open so swiftly and forcefully that it knocks into me.

"Hey . . . oww!" Stunned by the blast of pain, I stagger backward, clutching my forehead and wincing. "Oww, you just *killed* my head with that door!"

The door is opening the rest of the way, and then I see her.

Felicity.

She's wearing a long, dark gray dress and a plain white cotton cap that ties under her chin, just like the women in that pageant last night.

And she . . .

Wait a minute.

I thought Felicity Crane had legendary, blazing red hair. It was part of the evidence that had convicted her as a witch.

But the few strands of hair that are poking out from beneath her bonnet are what I would describe as colorless—a pale, nondescript blond. She must have dyed it during the trial.

But did they have hair coloring in those days?

Puzzled, I look her in the eye—and find myself gazing into the deepest, darkest black I've ever seen.

All I can think of as I stare into those bottomless eyes is that this girl is pure evil. It's actually radiating from her.

"Felicity," I start to say, but before I get the name out, she's moving forward, out of the secret cupboard, coming right at me. "Hey! What—?"

The next thing I know, she's given me a violent shove and sent me flying backward. I sprawl on the floor in disbelief as she glances around, then takes off through the passageway leading to the kitchen.

I'm so stunned that for a moment, all I can do is think about how much I hurt all over—my tailbone and my butt and my head, which is still throbbing from the door.

Then I realize what's happening—that she's getting away—and I force myself to my feet. I have to catch her.

I run through the kitchen and see that the back door is ajar. She must have run outside.

Scanning the yard, I expect to see her taking off in the direction of the woods. But she must be really fast, because there's already no sign of her.

Without stopping to think, I dash down the back steps and across the grass, keeping an eye out for Felicity.

I'm racing along the path through the trees when I realize what I've done—I've left the house while I'm grounded. And my father is right outside the front door. I'm going to get caught for sure.

But I don't stop and go back.

After all, he may already have realized I'm gone. And if I'm going to get into trouble, I might as well do it up right. At least this way, I'll be able to make contact with Zachariah.

I push further along the path, and the trees gradually give way to low shrubs and grass-covered dunes. Every dozen yards or so, I stop to listen for Felicity's footsteps.

And I keep wondering about her hostile behavior.

Why did she push me down? Why did she run away?

It doesn't make any sense, except that maybe she was so stunned by the time travel experience that she just freaked out.

And besides, if I were suddenly put on trial for witchcraft, and sentenced to death, I might be a little moody, too.

I'm scurrying along the path, my mind reeling, when suddenly, someone grabs me from behind.

I shriek and fight the sturdy grasp until I hear a familiar masculine voice near my ear. "Fret not, Abigail. 'Tis I, Zachariah Wellbourne."

"Zachariah!"

He lets go and I spin around to see him standing there.

"All day I have awaited thy arrival," he informs me, inspiring instant guilt.

"I'm sorry. I couldn't get away." I pause for a gasp of

breath and wipe the sweat away from my hairline. "My parents grounded me from last night."

He frowns. "Grounded?"

"Never mind," I pant, clutching my side. A sharp pain is jabbing just under my rib cage.

"Come and sit down," he says politely, taking my arm and leading me over to the little clearing nearby where we were last night.

As soon as I've sat and caught my breath, I say, "Zachariah, I saw Felicity."

His features brighten as soon as I mention her name. "My dear Felicity? Where?"

"Your 'dear' Felicity just materialized in the secret cupboard. Before I could talk to her, she ran away."

"She ran away? But why?"

"You tell me." Then I backtrack and start from the beginning, telling him how I heard her voice saying, "1963." I leave out the part about how she shoved me—all I say is that I got hit with the door.

"But one thing, Zachariah," I say when I've finished. "I thought Felicity was a redhead."

He nods, a faraway muse in his eyes. "She has glorious tresses, the flaming hue of trees in autumn . . . of a robin's breast . . . of—"

"Enough with the poetic waxing, already," I snap, cutting him off. "And anyway, the hair I saw didn't seem red. It was probably just some highlights, but . . ."

"Highlights?"

"Never mind. It looked blond, but I only saw a few strands."

"Blond?" He looks puzzled.

I guess he doesn't get it. I think for a moment, then try an archaic version of the word. "Flaxen?"

"Flaxen?"

I'm in pain and sweaty and right this minute my father is probably furious at me, and I'm not in the mood to play vocabulary games. I scowl and am about to speak when I think I hear something.

"What was that?" I ask Zachariah.

"Pardon?"

"Did you hear something? The grass rustling, or something? I think it came from over there."

"I heard nothing."

I listen again and hear a little breeze sifting through the grass.

That must be all it was.

Is it any wonder I'm a little jumpy, though? I've been through the wringer in the past few days.

"I knew Felicity would come after me," Zachariah is saying.

"Yeah, but I wonder how she got out of jail," I respond absently.

"Jail?" His horrified tone snaps me out of my distracted state. "Why is my Felicity in jail?"

"Oh, Zachariah . . ." I just stare at the panic on his face, wanting to kick myself. How could I have slipped like that?

But now that it's out, I have to tell him. I suppose he deserves to know the truth anyway. But I wish I didn't have to be the one who had to deliver the bad news.

I hold his hand gently while I tell him what happened to Felicity. As I tell the whole sad story, I keep thinking that there's something I'm forgetting. Something important.

By the time I get to the part where they sentenced Felicity to death, tears are streaming down his cheeks and he's shaking all over.

"And was she . . . executed?" he asks, watching me intently.

I just nod. He doesn't need to know any of the details. This is painful enough for him.

He lets out a horrible, wailing sob, and I put my arms around him, rocking him back and forth. When he finally calms down, he leaves his head on my shoulder and I stroke his shaggy hair.

"But who would do such a thing?" he asks in a desolate voice. "Who would accuse her of witchcraft? And why?"

"I can't remember the girl's name," I say truthfully. This is like déjà vu. Why can I never remember names when I need to?

"It was something old-fashioned," I add, then immediately think, what a stupid thing to say to someone from 1692—especially someone named Zachariah.

"And anyway, *who* accused her isn't important at this point," I conclude hurriedly. "What is important is that today is June twentieth, and Felicity was executed on June twenty-first. But if she's here, in the present—I mean, the future—then she can't be hung, can she?"

Zachariah doesn't reply. I pat his head. "Don't worry, Zachariah. We'll find—what was that?"

"What?"

I pull back from him and look over my shoulder. "Didn't you hear something? Footsteps?"

"No."

"Well, I did. And it came from over there." I point to the dunes nearby. I lower my voice to a whisper. "We have to go look."

He nods and sniffles, then we both stand up and tiptoe across the sandy clearing. We peer over the grasses that cover the dunes where I heard the sounds, and I brace myself, half expecting to see my father holding a bat.

But there's no one there—only more dunes, stretching for at least another mile toward the water.

I turn to Zachariah. "I wish I could stay here with you, but I can't. I have to get back home before I really get into trouble with my parents."

He nods, still looking bleak and dazed.

"Listen, Zachariah," I go, "you have to snap out of it. Felicity is going to be fine. She's here, isn't she? I'm sure she'll find you sooner or later. If I see her, I'll tell her where you are. Now I really have to get back."

"Yes," he says blankly, and sinks down onto the log again.

I give him one last hopeless look, then take off along the path, driven by overpowering self-preservation instincts.

Halfway home, I realize that I never finished telling Zachariah about Felicity's hair.

And I keep feeling like there's something else I should be remembering, but I can't put my finger on it.

Lately I have a brain like a sieve.

Up ahead, I can see that the back door of our house is still ajar.

There's a good sign.

I race toward it. As I sprint up the back steps, I can hear sawing noises and masculine voices coming from the front yard.

Could it be possible that my father didn't catch me after all?

Hoping against hope, I slip through the house to the front door and peek through the window.

My father is laughing at something Joe is saying as they carry a big plank over to a pile of boards under a tree.

If he'd noticed that I was missing, he wouldn't be joking around, would he?

Just to make sure, I open the door and call out, "Dad?"

He looks up. "Careful, Abbey! Back up a little."

He gestures and I look down. The front steps are gone entirely, and I'm perched on the edge of a drop that's at least six feet high. At the bottom, in the dirt, is a stack of old wooden planks, and even from here I can see that some of them have rusty nails facing up.

"Geez, what is this, some sort of trap?" I ask. "One false move and *ouch!* You get nailed in the keister."

Both Joe and Clarence laugh at that, and my father smiles.

He wouldn't be smiling at me if he knew I'd left the house, would he?

"So what did you want, Abbey?" he asks.

"Oh. Uh, I just wanted to see if anyone would like a cold Pepsi?"

Three sweaty, flushed faces brighten.

Everyone wants a cold Pepsi, so I go back into the kitchen. I grab three bottles from the refrigerator, hunt around for a bottle opener, pop off the tops, and go out the back door. I'm walking around to the front yard to hand out the drinks just as the Kennedys' car comes rolling up into the driveway.

Even from here, I can see that Mary Kennedy looks pretty grim when she spots me.

Uh-oh.

I guess my mother spilled the sordid tale of my wee-hour rendezvous with Riley.

I thrust all three bottles of Pepsi into Clarence's filthy hands, then sprint around to the back door.

By the time my mother comes in, I'm busily dusting in the keeping room.

"Hi, Mom," I say brightly. "Have a nice lunch?"

"Very nice."

"So, uh, what did you and Mrs. Kennedy talk about?" I sweep the dust cloth across a table and nearly knock over an ugly china figurine.

"Abbey, please be more careful," my mother says instantly, coming over and moving the figurine away from the edge of the table. "This is very valuable."

You've got to be kidding. It's hideous. But I'm already in enough trouble with her, so I just murmur, "Sorry."

"And if you're asking whether I told Mary about what happened last night, the answer is yes."

I stop dusting. "Oh."

"Yes. I thought she had a right to know what her son has been up to."

I don't say anything to that.

My mother's heels tap-tap-tap across the wooden floor, and I collapse miserably into a chair.

Can things possibly get any more dismal?

The twins chatter through supper about how they toured a boat marina today in day camp.

I just sit there glumly, pushing food around on my plate until my mother says, "Abbey, finish your casserole or no watermelon later."

Big deal—no watermelon, I think. The fact that she could even make such a stupid threat after everything I've been through makes me want to laugh.

As if not getting to eat watermelon is the worst thing that could happen to a person.

Abruptly, I put my fork down.

Everyone looks at me.

"I'm not hungry," I inform them.

My mother starts to protest, "But you love tuna casserole, Abbey, and—"

"Grace, she's a big girl. She knows whether she's hungry or not," my father cuts in abruptly. He turns to me and goes, "If you're done eating, then you can march right outside and move the garbage cans out to the pit for me. I'm going to burn trash tonight."

"Fine." Anything would be better than sitting at this table with everyone nagging me.

Even lugging smelly trash cans around.

I push back my chair and march out the back door.

Right before I bang it closed behind me, I hear Peter say worriedly, "What's the matter with Abbey?"

"Nothing," my mother tells him. "Eat your casserole and then we'll cut the watermelon."

I stomp over to the two gray metal cans by the door and lug the first one across the grass to the trash pit.

I'm almost there with the second can when I hear a footstep behind me.

Before I can turn, strong arms grab me.

I cry out and jerk my head around.

I'm expecting to see Zachariah.

Or Felicity.

But it's not either of them.

It's Riley Kennedy.

FOURTEEN

"Hey, New Yo-*awk*," Riley says in a low voice. "What's going on?"

I just stare at him, trying frantically to figure out what to tell him.

Instinctively, I play dumb to buy time. "What do you mean?"

"I mean, supposedly you and I were sneaking around together last night. What were we up to?"

Gradually, I'm noticing that for some reason, he doesn't look angry. Just curious. And maybe even amused.

"What do you mean, what were we up to?" I ask, looking over my shoulder to make sure my parents won't be able to spot Riley.

They can't possibly see us. There's a clump of bushes concealing this spot from the house.

"Did we have a good time?" He flashes that Riley grin at me and bobs his eyebrows under the brim of his Red Sox cap.

I put my hands on my hips. "Riley . . ."

He follows suit and mimics me. "Abbey . . ."

"Come on, listen to me."

"I'm all ears."

"I'm really sorry. I didn't mean to get you into trouble.

I'll tell your mother that you aren't lying, that you really didn't meet me, and—"

"Oh, she doesn't think I'm lying."

"Huh?"

"She doesn't think that because I didn't deny anything. I just went along with it."

I'm stunned. "You *what?*"

"I went along with it. I figured, for a nice girl like you to make up a story like that . . . well, you must have had a really good reason."

"I did." I just stare at him. "I can't believe you covered for me."

He shrugs.

"Are you in big trouble?" I ask.

"Nah. I'm eighteen. I'm going away to college in a few months. What are they going to do, ground me?"

"Mine did."

"You're a girl."

I'm instantly annoyed. "So?"

"So, girls shouldn't be sneaking around in the middle of the night. And while we're on the subject, why *were* you sneaking around?"

"I can't tell you."

"Does it have anything to do with the weird guy you saw the other night?"

My jaw drops. "How do you know about—oh, that's right. You were eavesdropping when I was telling Katie."

He doesn't deny it, just stands there waiting for an answer. Finally, he goes, "Well?"

"Riley," I say, suddenly weary of all the lies, "if I tell you this, you have to promise that you won't tell a single soul. No one."

"I promise," he says, and the teasing expression is gone. He looks earnest—even concerned.

What a relief it will be to share this with him. Maybe he can even help somehow.

"Okay, here's what happened." I take a deep breath. "I was—"

"Abbey?" my father calls suddenly from the house.

We both jump.

I peer around the bushes and see my father standing in the back doorway.

"Yeah, Dad?"

"Come'ere."

"Okay," I call, then turn back to whisper to Riley, "don't you dare move. If they catch me talking to you out here, I'm dead."

He nods, and I hurry back through the dusk toward the house.

My parents and the twins are in the kitchen, opening drawers and cupboards, apparently hunting for something.

"Abbey," my father says as soon as I walk in, "have you seen the meat cleaver?"

"The meat cleaver?" I glance over to the block of knives on the counter. Handles of all sizes are sticking out, but the big slot at the top where the cleaver belongs is empty.

"I just went to get it so I could use it to cut into the watermelon rind," my father explains, "and it's gone."

"Well, I didn't take it," I say crankily. "Why do I always get blamed for everything around here?"

"No one's *blaming* you, Abbey," my mother says, getting down on her hands and knees and looking under the table. "We just thought you might know where it is."

"Well, I don't."

"It was here this afternoon," my father is saying, shaking

his head. "I saw it when I took out the bread knife to cut the rolls for lunch."

"I really have to clean this floor," my mother mutters from under the table. "There are crumbs all over the place, and . . . what is this?"

I notice her hand reaching up, putting something she found on top of the table.

I glance away, then do a double-take.

It's a dried-up bunch of leaves and stems.

I stare at it, then look at my father and brothers.

Dad is going through the silverware drawer for probably the tenth time, and the twins are involved in a typical shoving match.

Swiftly and casually, I move forward and scoop the dried leaves off the table.

"I don't understand. The cleaver couldn't just walk away by itself," my mother tells us, crawling backward, standing up and brushing off her knees.

She glances at the table, then looks vaguely puzzled, like she's wondering what happened to the clump of leaves she just put there.

To distract her, I quickly say, "Hey, is that it?" I point to the block of knives on the counter.

Everyone looks in that direction.

"Oops, no, I guess not. That's just a steak knife, isn't it. Well, anyway, don't worry. It'll turn up."

"I'm sure it will, sooner or later, but I need it to cut into this watermelon right now." My father thumps the hard green rind.

"I'm not in the mood for melon anymore, anyway," my mother says, wiping her drooping hair out of her eyes. She seems to have forgotten all about the leaves she found on the floor.

"Maybe someone stole the cleaver," Peter says in a frightened voice.

"That's stupid," Paul scornfully replies. "Robbers want money and gold and jewels. Who the heck would steal a stupid cleaver?"

Yeah, who the heck would steal a stupid cleaver? my mind echoes absently as I clutch the dried herbs behind my back . . .

And then suddenly, my blood runs cold.

About five minutes have passed.

I'm still just standing here, like I'm in a daze.

Around me, my family has given up searching for the cleaver and is deciding that no one is in the mood for watermelon anymore, anyway.

"Why don't we drive out to Super Cone on 1A and get ice cream?" my mother suggests, keeping an eye on Peter, who still looks worried from Paul's comment about robbers.

Instantly, both of the twins shout, "Yeah! Ice cream!"

And even my father says, "Good idea. While we're out that way, we can stop by the hardware store. It's open till nine. I want to see if they got that shipment of lumber in yet. We can't make any progress on the front steps until we have it."

"All right, then, boys go get your windbreakers on—it's getting chilly. And, Abbey, you find a jacket, too. You must be freezing in that sleeveless blouse. And you might want to change into some long pants, too."

"Uh, I'm not coming."

My mother looks surprised. "You don't want ice cream?"

I keep one hand behind my back, fingering the dried leaves. "No, thanks. I'll just stay here."

My parents exchange a glance, and then my father says sternly, "I don't want any nonsense from you, young lady. If you stay here, you're not to set foot outside of this house. And I mean it."

"Geez, Dad, what do you think I am?" I ask, instantly offended. "You've taken me prisoner, okay? I'm not going anyplace."

"I don't like that tone, young lady. And just to keep you busy while we're gone, your mother is going to give you a chore. Grace?"

She thinks for a moment, then says, "You can sweep the kitchen floor for me. Then you can sort the laundry in the hampers upstairs and start a load of whites. Then you can dust all the furniture upstairs. And the tub needs to be scrubbed, and you can clean the sink and toilet, too, while you're at it."

Do you believe this?

"Geez, who am I, Cinderella?" I mutter.

"What was that remark?" That's my father, whose patience is clearly wearing thin.

"Nothing."

"I expect everything to be accomplished by the time we come back home, Abigail. Do you understand?"

I look him in the eye. "Yes. I understand."

"Good."

And he turns and jingles his car keys as the twins come back in, wearing their matching blue-and-white striped windbreakers. "All set, boys?" he asks them cheerfully, reaching out to pat their stubbly heads.

Suddenly, I think about how he used to ruffle my hair and tease me and call me "Abbey-my-girl." It seems like a long time ago.

"I miss home," I say impulsively to no one in particular.

"I wish we'd never come here. I hate Seacliffe, and I hate this house."

Everyone looks at me, surprised.

Then my mother says, "Oh, Abbey, don't be ridiculous. Every other summer, you've complained about being stuck in the city."

"Well, I wish I was back there right now." I sound like I'm on the verge of tears and I'm fighting to swallow a painful lump that's suddenly tightening my throat. "It isn't fair that I have to be stuck here."

My father shakes his head and says, "Well, you'd better get used to it, because you've still got a few months to go before you're back in New York."

Then they all walk out the door, going to get their ice cream.

"Lock the door behind us, Abbey," my mother calls over her shoulder.

I just stand there, feeling like a big baby as the hot tears that have welled up in my eyes spill over. It feels good to cry, and I really go at it for a few minutes.

I think about everything that's happened since we got to Seacliffe.

The whole mess with Zachariah.

The stupid argument with Katie.

Finding out that Brian cheated on me.

Having to lie about sneaking around with Riley.

Getting grounded by my parents.

The way Felicity shoved me.

Having to work like a slave around the house.

What a lousy summer this is turning out to be!

"I hate it here," I announce emphatically to the empty kitchen, bringing my hand up to wipe my wet cheeks.

And that's when I realize that I'm still clutching the dried leaves my mother found on the floor.

I move them in front of my nose and sniff.

Even though I'm stuffed up from crying, I catch a whiff of a distinctly pungent, woodsy scent.

It's not like anything I've ever smelled before.

This has to be the bunch of herbs Zachariah brought with him. He must have dropped it on the kitchen floor as he was running out of the house that first night.

I have to put these somewhere for safekeeping.

The secret cupboard, I decide without hesitation. That's the only place where I can be sure that no one in my family will find them.

Still sniffling, but feeling infinitely better, I hurry into the keeping room and open the closet beside the fireplace.

I reach up and feel around the ceiling for the hidden lever.

"Eeeeuuuhh!" My hand has just brushed something soft and filmy—cobwebs. "There better not be any spiders up there," I mutter to myself.

Then I stop. Did I just hear something behind me?

Several things happen simultaneously.

I belatedly remember that I forgot to lock the kitchen door . . .

I start to turn around . . .

My fingers find the lever and the secret door springs forward . . .

I realize I'm not alone . . .

And I discover, with sheer and numbing horror, exactly what happened to the missing meat cleaver.

FIFTEEN

"Please," I say in a tiny, trembling voice. "Please don't hurt me with that."

She doesn't say a word, just stands there with the cleaver raised, staring at me with those bottomless black eyes. I can feel hatred radiating into me.

"Please . . ." I sound plaintive now. I've got to get control of myself; I've got to hold her off by distracting her. "Where did you get that cleaver?" I ask, even though I already understand what must have happened.

When I ran into the kitchen after her this afternoon, she wasn't already out the door, as I thought. She must have concealed herself someplace in the kitchen, and after I ran out toward the woods, she grabbed the knife from the counter. I wasn't following her along that path . . . she was following me.

And now I've got to get away from her somehow.

But I'm in the closet and she's blocking the doorway, not speaking, just staring at me with those glittering, colorless eyes.

It's hopeless.

But I have to try.

"Please, Felicity . . . why are you doing this?"

"Felicity?" She gives a short, harsh laugh. "I am not Felicity."

"Then, who are you?" I ask, even as it dawns on me.

The elusive thing I kept trying so hard to remember.

Now it all comes back to me, and everything makes sense.

Zachariah and Jemima weren't the only two people who mysteriously disappeared from Seacliffe in 1692. Someone else did, too . . . the girl who had accused Felicity of witchcraft.

I remember her name, then, and the last puzzle piece clatters into place.

It's Elspeth Andrewes.

"How dare thee?" she's asking me, her voice low with venom. "He is mine. I have loved him since we were children. *How dare thee?*"

"What are you talking about?"

"I saw thee locked in an embrace with Zachariah Wellbourne," she spits out.

"With Zachariah . . . ? I was only comforting him, Elspeth." My mind is racing.

She's insane. And she's dangerous.

I stare, mesmerized, at the gleaming silver blade that's only inches from my face.

"Comforting him?" She narrows her gaze. "For what reason?"

"He was upset . . ." I trail off. I don't want to say the wrong thing and set her off.

"Upset? Why?" She gestures slightly with the blade, as if to remind me that it's there—and she'll use it.

"Because he found out what happened to Felicity," I say truthfully, riveted on the cleaver.

"Ah . . . Felicity Crane. His 'beloved,' " she says mockingly. "She will no longer stand in my way. She will hang at dawn tomorrow."

"But why?"

"Felicity Crane is a witch!" she says harshly. "I saw her with my own eyes, through the window on that night."

"What did you see?" I whisper.

"I saw her cause my dear Zachariah to vanish. She sent him here, to the future. I heard her words as she told him how to use the herbs, how to close his eyes and concentrate. I heard him utter the year, '1963.' And then she opened the door, and he was gone. 'Twas then that I came forward with my accusation." She laughs bitterly. "She tried to deny it, but 'twas no use. Now she will die. And now, I have come here to find Zachariah, to make him mine at last."

"But, Elspeth—"

"And what do I find?" Her eyes are boring into mine. "I find *thee*. Stroking my Zachariah's hair, clutching him to thy bosom . . ." Her voice is trembling with barely controlled rage.

"Elspeth," I say desperately, trying to reason with her. My fingers are clammy around the bunch of dried herbs. "I barely know Zachariah. I'm not in love with him."

"Thy words are lies!"

"No, I'm not lying. Please, don't hurt me with that."

But a wicked smile is settling over her features. And she's raising the arm that holds the knife.

In one frantic instant, I make a decision.

Lunging forward, I give her a violent shove.

Instead of falling backward, she only stumbles against the door frame, catching it to break her fall.

There's still no escape—I can't get by her.

In a panic, I scramble for my only option.

Reaching backward, still clutching the dried leaves in my fingers, I grab the edge of the secret cupboard door and pull it out far enough so that I can slip inside. I tug on the coarse rope tied to the other side and the door bangs shut behind me, the catch mechanism clicking into place.

Through the thick wood, I can hear her muffled exclamation.

Now she's in a rage, clawing at the door, trying to open it, apparently forgetting about the secret lever above.

But she's going to figure it out any second now.

If I don't do this, I'll be dead.

I don't have a choice.

Standing in the exact center of the closet, I pray that the pentagram still works. Then I crumble several of the brittle leaves between my fingers, letting the powdery bits fall to the floor.

I squeeze my eyes shut and concentrate, repeating over and over again, "1962, 1962, 1962 . . ."

It has to work. It *has* to.

I'm going to be able to open that door, step out into the keeping room, and discover that Elspeth is gone and it's June twentieth, last year.

Please, please let this work . . .

I'm frantic.

"1962, 1692, 1962, 1962, 1692 . . ."

And just as I realize that my tongue keeps twisting around the numbers, it happens.

I feel a tingling sensation zapping through me, and a roaring sound, like rushing wind, fills my ears.

Tentatively, I open my eyes and listen intently.

The clawing sounds on the other side of the door have stopped.

So has the tingling.

And the roaring inside my head.

All I see is blackness, and all I hear is silence.

Hardly daring to breathe, I reach out and push against the door.

When it doesn't open, I have to fight back a sudden attack of claustrophobia.

I'm trapped in here! Oh, God, I'm trapped. I can't—

Wait a minute.

Zachariah said something about a secret latch on this side, too.

I reach up and feel around in the crack where the top of the door meets the ceiling. For a few minutes, I'm so pre-occupied with the search that I don't think about anything else.

Then I locate a small wooden bump, jiggle it, and the door in front of me springs forward.

As soon as it happens, I freeze. My knees feel like they're going to buckle. All I can do is wonder what I'll find when I open the closet door.

Can it possibly be 1962? Will I find Great-Uncle William dozing in the old recliner in front of the television set?

Or maybe it's still 1963, and Elspeth is hiding out there, waiting to lunge at me with the cleaver.

The thought makes me shudder, and I think that anything would be better than that.

Even 1692.

But surely just because I got confused and said the wrong year once or twice, I didn't send myself back almost three hundred years.

Even though that's exactly what happened to Zacha-riah . . .

Even though I felt the tingling at the exact moment I said 1692 . . .

No.

Taking a deep breath, I push the first door open, then take a few steps forward, into the dark, cramped closet beside the fireplace.

"Here goes," I whisper to myself, and push on the second door.

It swings open with a creaking noise.

At first, there's only more darkness.

Then gradually, as my gaze grows accustomed, I can see shapes and shadows in the dim light of dusk that spills through the paned windows. My eyes trace the outlines of unfamiliar furniture . . . and over there, between the windows—is that a spinning wheel?

I gasp, and try to breathe calmly, but my nose is assaulted by strange odors. The air in here is unbearably close and stale, and tinged heavily with woodsmoke and grease. Those distinct smells mingle with the ever-present salty scent of the sea and the faint stench of manure wafting in on a hot breeze.

I've got to get out of here!

I turn instinctively toward the narrow passage I know will lead me to the kitchen and the back door. But the moment I try to move through it, my foot knocks into something that makes a terrible clatter. Looking down, I see that I've kicked over some type of metal bucket filled with grain.

Almost instantly, I hear startled exclamations and footsteps overhead.

I desperately want to move—I have to flee!—but I'm frozen to the spot.

Vaguely, I listen to the voices upstairs.

I'm so dizzy . . .

Get out. . . . Hurry . . .

I command my feet to move, but somehow they won't, and I feel as though I'm swaying.

And then suddenly, the footsteps are pounding down the stairs, the room is tilting crazily, and the hard wooden floor is rushing up to meet my face.

I slowly drift back to consciousness, aware only that my forehead feels like it's splitting open and I'm sweating. It's unbearably hot and humid . . .

Why am I bundled up beneath a blanket?

Oh my God . . .

My eyes snap open, and simultaneously, it all comes back to me.

I'm in 1692.

At first, all I can see is flickering candlelight against the dark, low ceiling overhead. But I hear voices muttering nearby, and turn my head slightly in that direction. Instantly a wave of pain throbs through my skull, so intense that I gasp.

"She awakens!" someone says excitedly, and suddenly a ring of faces are looming over me, none of them familiar. Some of them belong to children.

"What say thee?" booms a man with a deeply wrinkled face.

Dazed, I feel my eyes starting to close again. Someone kicks me in the side, and I force them to stay open.

Again, the booming voice says, "What say thee?"

I realize he's talking to me, and I open my mouth to answer, but only a croak comes out. I feel like I'm burning up, trapped beneath a musty blanket or quilt of some sort. I have to get it off. Carefully, I move my arm out from beneath it, and as soon as I do, they all gasp and step back.

"Cover thyself, witch," says a different male voice. "Do not dare offend our eyes with thy bare skin."

Someone reaches down and flips the quilt back over my arm.

Frustrated, I feel sweat—and maybe blood—dripping from my hairline.

Then I realize what he just said. *Cover thyself, witch.*

Witch.

Surely these people don't think . . .

"What say thee in thy defense?" That's the booming voice again.

I'm so stunned I still can't reply. It's dawning on me that this is 1692, and for some reason, these people think I'm a witch.

And I know what happened to accused witches in 1692.

I have to tell them they're wrong. "Please . . ." I say, and as soon as I speak I hear a woman cry out.

"I beg of thee, Goody Crane, remove thyself and thy children from this chamber," a man in a broad-brimmed hat says.

"Do as the reverend asks, Martha," says a somber-looking man.

"But, Josiah—"

"Martha, go!"

"Very well," the woman says. She sounds like she's on the verge of hysteria as she herds the group of children out of the room.

As they go, I hear a child ask, "Mother, is that girl a witch as my sister Felicity is?"

His sister Felicity? Josiah? Goody Crane?

In horror, I realize that these people are Felicity's family. Of course they are—this would be their house.

But if their own daughter was wrongly accused of witchcraft, maybe they'll be understanding and help me.

"Reverend Griggs," says the man with the booming voice, "we must remove this witch from the dwelling, for she may bring harm to the family of Josiah. He and the Goodwife Crane hath suffered enough. Tomorrow morning at dawn, their own daughter, Felicity, will hang on the gallows for witchcraft."

"Speak not of that witch as my daughter!" the somber Josiah bites out. "She is no daughter of mine."

I can't believe my ears. Did Felicity's family actually disown her when she was accused?

"Thou hast my sympathy, Josiah," says the reverend before turning his attention back to me. "Hast thou any words to speak in thy defense?"

"Yes," I say desperately. "I'm not a witch. Please, you've got to believe me."

"If thou were not sent to Seacliffe to do the devil's work, then how might thou explain thy strange garments?"

I frantically realize that I'm wearing a sleeveless blouse and Bermuda shorts. "I traveled here from another place, a place where these kinds of clothes are the fashion," I say feebly.

"And what of the gleaming talisman encircling thy neck?"

"Gleaming talisman . . . ?" What the heck is he talking about?

Then I realize that he must mean my Beatles pendant. Oh, Lord, how am I going to explain that?

I don't even want to try. I'll only end up convincing them that I'm guilty.

Not that it matters anyway.

Because I just remembered something else that I had forgotten.

Something that happened in June of 1692 in Seacliffe.

Something so horrifying that I can't even think about it.

But the monotonous words of that pageant narrator are echoing through my mind.

*An unfamiliar young woman appeared in Seacliffe . . . she
was dressed in strange, exotic robes and adorned with magic
charms. . . . Within twenty-four hours of Felicity Crane's execution, she was convicted of witchcraft . . . and hung. To this
day, her identity remains a mystery.*

Well, it's not a mystery anymore.

The stranger—the second witch convicted and hung in
Seacliffe in June, 1692—was me, Abigail Harmon.

SIXTEEN

The next time I come to, I'm aware that somehow, the hard floor beneath my back is repeatedly jerking and rattling.

I open my eyes and realize that it's not the floor at all. They must have moved me to some kind of wagon or cart. I can hear clopping hooves and wheels bumping over rough ground.

It's still night, and above me the sky is filled with stars. I can hear waves crashing nearby, and the hot, muggy air smells like a mixture of algae, rotting fish, and mud. We seem to be in the woods—there are trees all around, and every so often what seems to be clusters of leaves from low branches brush against my face.

As the full realization of what's happening comes rushing back at me, I breathe the warm, rank air deeply, willing myself not to pass out again. Staying alert is my only hope.

I have to get away!

Panicking, I try to sit up, but for some reason, I can't move my arms . . . or my legs. They seem banded at the wrists and ankles, as if they've tied me up.

Gradually, my terror is replaced by fury. How dare they do this to me!

"Hey!" I try to shout, but my voice is drowned out by the rattling cart and the horses' hooves. I clear my throat and try again. "Hey!" I scream at the top of my lungs.

"The prisoner speaketh, Reverend Griggs," says a booming nearby voice. I crane my neck, wincing against the splitting pain in my head, and see the silhouettes of two men seated on a bench at the front of the cart.

"What sayeth thee?" asks the reverend, slowing the horses.

"I demand to know where you're taking me!"

"We are transporting thee to the prison in Seacliffe."

"Why? I didn't commit any crime."

"Thou hast been accused of witchcraft."

"I'm not a witch!" I shriek in total frustration. I kick my bound legs repeatedly against the side of the cart for emphasis.

"Silence!" says the other man, the one with the booming voice.

I feel like I'm about to lose it entirely. "How dare you accuse me of being a witch! How *dare* you!" I grate out through clenched teeth. "I've done nothing wrong."

" 'Tis up to the magistrate to determine thy crimes," is the only reply, and then he clicks his tongue and urges the horses to go faster.

In despair, I squeeze my eyes closed and pray more fervently than I ever have before in my life, reciting every prayer I ever learned in Sunday School and begging God to save me.

Suddenly, from the bench up front, I hear the booming voiced man say, "Hark ye, Reverend Griggs. The prisoner speaketh the Lord's Prayer."

"That cannot be, Ezekiel. 'Tis common knowledge that no servant of the devil is able to speak the Lord's Prayer."

"I'm *not* a servant of the devil!" I holler. "Listen, I'll say it again. Our Father, who art in heaven . . ." And I rapidly spit out the entire prayer. Except that I'm so agitated that my tongue gets twisted at the end and I stumble a little.

"She is unable to say the prayer without error," the reverend says triumphantly. "She hath proven herself to be the devil's servant."

"I have not!" I scream, desperately thrusting my arms, trying to break the ties. But the coarse rope burns into my wrists, and my entire body seems racked with pain.

Miserably, I stop trying to get free. I just lie there sobbing pitifully as the wagon keeps moving forward.

Mosquitos keep buzzing around me, and every time they land on my face or neck and start biting, I instinctively try to move my hand to slap them away. But the rope makes that impossible, so all I can do is let them attack me. At least the rest of my body is covered by this mangy old quilt, even though I'm soaked in sweat beneath it. It must be at least a hundred degrees out.

Eventually, we seem to be emerging from the woods. I sense more open spaces around us, and I can see the occasional outline of a peaked roof above.

Then the horses slow to a stop and I hear the men getting off their bench. They come around back, and the next thing I know, I'm being roughly jerked into the air and carried into a dank, stone structure nearby.

Another man, one they call Benjamin, appears and, carrying a candle, leads the way along an unlit passageway. He's holding a ring of keys, and he stops in front of what looks like a cell.

The next thing I know, an iron-barred door is swinging open, and I'm being deposited on the dirt floor behind it.

I'm momentarily relieved when I feel them cutting the ropes that are digging into my ankles. I flex my toes, which are tingling and numb from the lack of circulation.

Then I freeze, hearing chains being dragged across the floor. I look down in horror and see that they're attaching heavy iron shackles to my legs.

"No!" I scream, kicking wildly. "Stop it! Let me go!"

"Restrain her, Ezekiel!"

Strong arms grab me from behind, and a smelly hand clamps over my mouth. It's blocking my nose, and I can't breathe.

I can't breathe!

Everything grows blurry and fades to black.

The next time I open my eyes, I'm alone and flickering candlelight is filtering into the cell from somewhere nearby, casting eerie shadows.

I gradually realize that I'm sprawled on the dirt floor and something is tickling my arm, which seems to be pinned to the wall above me.

I glance up and scream.

My hand is cuffed to the wall, and an enormous centipede is crawling across my forearm. I instinctively flail to get it off, and wince in pain as the shackle holds my wrist in place and I pull a muscle in my shoulder.

"Oww," I wail, feeling tears spilling over my cheeks. "Please help me," I whimper. "Please, somebody . . ."

And then I hear a voice.

A soothing, female voice.

And it's coming from nearby.

Startled, I turn my head and see that there's another cell just beyond the iron bars of mine.

Inside it is a girl about my age.

"Do not weep," she's saying quietly to me. "It will do thee no good."

She's dressed in rags, and dirt is streaked across her face. She's painfully thin and her eyes are so sunken that I can barely see them. And her hair is matted and filthy . . .

But even in the dim light I can see that it's a glorious shade of red.

"Felicity?" I ask in a hushed voice.

"Aye, I am Felicity Crane." She peers at me through the darkness. "Thou is aware of my name. Yet I know thee not."

"I'm Abbey," I whisper across the dank corridor separating us. "We've never met, but I know who you are."

"How can that be?"

I can't tell her the truth—that I came from the future, where she's infamous as the first witch executed in Seacliffe.

Instead, I just sniffle and say, "Zachariah Wellbourne described you to me."

As soon as she hears his name, she scrambles as close to the bars as her shackles will let her go. "Thou hast seen my beloved Zachariah?"

"Yes."

"Where?"

For a moment, I don't answer her.

Then I take a deep breath. I might as well tell her the truth now. What's the point of lying? "In 1963."

She's silent for a few seconds, as though she's gathering her thoughts. Then she says simply, "Thou hast come here from the future?"

"Yes."

"And my Zachariah was there?"

"Yes."

She looks relieved. "He is safe, then?"

"Safe? Yes, he's safe." *I hope,* I add silently, remembering that that psycho Elspeth is on the loose with a cleaver.

"How did thou come to be here?"

"It's a long story," I tell her.

"I haven't much time, for I am to be executed for witchcraft with the first light of dawn," is her straightforward reply.

"Oh, Felicity, that's so unfair!" I feel like I'm going to start crying again, for her and for myself. "There has to be a way out."

"No. I have been found guilty and sentenced to death. They will not hear my pleas of innocence. But do not pity me. I am truly quite relieved that death is near, for it will bring peace from the suffering and squalor I have endured in this wretched prison. But I wish I could cast my eyes upon the face of my beloved Zachariah one last time, and tell him that I love him."

"He knows that," I say around a monster lump in my throat. Tears are starting to trickle down my face again.

I have to pull myself together. She's the one who's about to die, and she seems resigned to it, even serene.

I'm the one who's falling apart.

"I believe he does know," Felicity tells me. Then she adds fervently, "But wilt thou tell him for me?"

"I would tell him if I could, but I don't think I'll be seeing him again."

"Speak quickly, for my time is running out. How did thee come to be here?"

I start talking, spilling the whole story to her, leaving out the part about how her own fate is a legend in Seacliffe.

As soon as I get to the part about Elspeth, she bursts out, "No! She must not find my beloved Zachariah! She is evil! 'Twas Elspeth Andrewes who accused me of witchcraft," she adds bitterly.

"I know."

"Too late, I realized that she had been hidden beneath the window the night I sent Zachariah through time. She came forward and attacked me, threatening to kill me. She was babbling about Zachariah, telling me that he loved her and that she would go to him after she had destroyed me."

"She's trying," I tell her. "And she attacked me, too. She thought Zachariah and I were lovers—but we're not, of course," I assure Felicity hurriedly. "He's pining away for you, Felicity."

Suddenly, a door is thrown open down the corridor, and we both hear footsteps approaching.

Three tall figures appear, all of them wearing dark hoods and carrying lanterns. The flickering light illuminates Felicity's cell, and for the first time I can see her eyes.

They're a vivid blue—and they're wide with fear.

She turns to me as one of the hooded men unlocks the iron-barred door to her cell.

"Abbey," she says desperately, "thou must survive somehow. Do not let them condemn thee to the same fate."

I can't speak. I'm paralyzed with horror, watching as the men enter her cell.

The shortest of the three unlocks the shackles that bind her wrists to the wall. Swiftly, he produces a length of rope from the folds of his robe, jerks her arms behind her back, and roughly ties them together at the wrists.

Then another man steps forward and says, "Rise, Felicity Crane. The hour of thy death is upon thee."

I recognize the booming voice as belonging to one of the men who captured me last night.

Before Felicity can respond, she's yanked roughly to her feet.

She stands there bravely as another man comes down the corridor and enters the cell. He's wearing a long black robe, but no hood. He unrolls a scroll of paper and reads a list of charges against Felicity.

". . . and thus," he concludes, "thou hast been condemned by the good and God-fearing people of Seacliffe to die on this twenty-first day of June in the year of our Lord sixteen hundred and ninety-two. Hast thou any last words to utter?"

She pulls herself up straight and looks him in the eye. "Only that I am innocent."

He stares at her for a moment, then spits in her face.

She doesn't flinch.

He turns to the three hooded men and says, "Carry on," before he turns and walks away.

"Abbey," Felicity calls out in a clear voice just before a crude hood is pulled over her head.

I catch a last glimpse of her big blue eyes.

They're pleading with me.

"Please, Abbey . . . please get back to my Zachariah somehow. Please tell him that I love him, and that my dying thoughts shall be of him. Someday we will find each other again."

In a choked voice, I whisper, "I promise, Felicity."

"God keep thee, Abbey . . ."

Then I watch helplessly as, hooded and dragging the chains from the shackles still fastened around her ankles, Felicity Crane is led to the gallows.

SEVENTEEN

"I will ask thee only once more . . . state thy name."

I stare mutely at the man seated at the front of the courtroom and shake my head. I'm not about to say a single word.

I don't know if I could speak even if I wanted to. I'm still reeling from what I saw as they marched me over the town commons to the courthouse.

I know it was the commons, even though it looked nothing like Seacliffe today. There was only a big dusty area with a few trees and patches of yellowish grass here and there. Livestock—chickens and goats and pigs—were roaming everywhere. And the buildings around it looked like little more than shacks, except for a church that I vaguely recognized.

There were people milling everywhere, dressed in heavy dark clothing despite the blazing sun. They jumped back and gave me plenty of space when I was marched through. Most of them shielded their eyes from me, but the few who caught my gaze looked at me with a mixture of fear and hate. Some of them spit at me, and called me a witch or the "devil's servant."

But that wasn't what disturbed me.

It was the tree I glimpsed just before I was shoved inside the courthouse. A piece of rope that had been hacked off at the bottom dangled from one of the branches. On the ground below it was a crude wooden platform and a pile of dirt where a grave was apparently still being dug.

And next to that was a long, lumpy object bundled in a drab gray blanket.

Even from several yards away, I could see the flash of brilliant red glinting in the sunlight—a lock of hair that had slipped out from beneath the shroud.

"Oh, Felicity, no," I murmured, closing my eyes against the chilling sight.

And then I was dragged into this low-ceilinged room lined with wooden benches, and made to stand in the front as curious townspeople filtered in and took their places. Along one side is a row of male jurors whose expressions make it only too clear that in their minds, I'm already convicted.

Now this roomful of Puritans is gawking at me, and the man they call the chief justice is waiting for an answer.

But he's not going to get one.

Finally, he turns to the man who is seated nearby, poised with a quill and paper. "She will not reveal her name. Refer to her in court documents as 'the prisoner.' "

The man nods, dips the quill into a pot of ink, and writes something.

A magistrate steps forward. "The prisoner appeared late on the evening last—the twentieth of June, the year of our Lord sixteen hundred and ninety-two—in the home of Josiah Crane. How came this to pass? Goodman Crane?"

A man I recognize as Felicity's father stands up in the back of the courtroom and walks forward. He looks pale, and I wonder if he watched as his own daughter was hung only a few hours ago.

For a fleeting moment, I think that maybe he'll be so shaken by what happened to her that he'll refuse to answer their questions now.

Then I remember that he testified against Felicity, and I want to shout that I think he's a despicable little weasel.

He stands in front of the magistrate and judge, clears his throat, and fiddles nervously with the black hat he's clutching.

Finally, he begins to speak in a feeble voice. "My wife, our children, and I had retired to the bedchambers on the second story of our dwelling when we did hear a terrible racket from the keeping room below. We—"

"Speak up, Goodman Crane!"

He clears his throat again and his voice gets a fraction louder. "We hurried down to investigate and discovered this young stranger slumped, nearly naked, on the floor. I sent my eldest boy, John, to fetch a blanket from the barn so that we might conceal her flesh from our eyes. I then dispatched John to alert the Reverend Griggs and our neighbor, Ezekiel Browne. When they returned, the stranger was stirring and regaining consciousness. 'Twas then that we realized the prisoner hath familiarity with the devil."

He turns up the volume on the last part and turns toward me. I can feel dozens of hateful eyes boring into me. I try to tune Josiah out as he goes on with his account of my arrival.

It's sweltering in this room because of the crowd and the temperature outside, and the stench of B.O. is overpowering. I'm wearing some foul-smelling dress they forced me to put over my clothes, and my hair is disgustingly matted and filthy.

I keep feeling as though I'm going to faint. I haven't eaten anything today. They brought me some slimy greenish water and a crust of moldy bread in my cell, but I refused it.

Josiah Crane has stopped talking, and I look over to see that he's looking expectantly at the magistrate.

"The court thanks thee for thy testimony. Return to thy seat, Goodman Crane. Goodman Browne will now come forward."

I see the tall man from last night—the one with the booming voice—approaching. I narrow my eyes and stare at him.

I find a flash of satisfaction in the fact that he looks frightened of me, and carefully stays back, way over on the opposite side of the judge.

"What say thee, Goodman Browne?" asks the magistrate.

When Ezekiel Browne opens his mouth to speak, his voice comes out in a pathetic little squeak. Someone titters in the back of the room.

Then he clears his throat, and is back to his usual booming self. "The Reverend Griggs and I transported the prisoner from the Crane dwelling to the prison. 'Twas then that the good reverend and I witnessed evidence of her deviltry. The prisoner attempted to utter the Lord's Prayer, but was unable to do so without stumbling over the words."

A gasp goes up in the courtroom.

The magistrate turns an evil smile on me. " 'Tis widely known that no witch can recite the Lord's Prayer without stumbling," he announces. "But the prisoner—"

That does it. I've had it. I'll show them.

Cutting him off in midsentence, I open my mouth and begin speaking slowly and carefully, enunciating every word. "Our father, who art in heaven . . ."

I say the entire Lord's prayer flawlessly from beginning to end.

When I'm finished, I stand there, waiting.

The courtroom is hushed for a moment.

Then a woman stands up in the back of the courtroom. I recognize her as Sarah Crane, Felicity's mother. "The devil himself was giving the prisoner her cues!" she cries out. "I saw him—a horrible black figure. He was hovering there, in the corner, beyond Goodman Browne."

Instantly there's an uproar. A few people flee, children are whimpering, and a woman faints.

I just stand here, stunned.

How can they believe her? How can they think the devil appeared?

"I saw him, too!" hollers a man in the front row, and a few others join in, pointing to the corner behind Ezekiel Browne, who is now cowering in fear.

These people are insane. That's all there is to it.

I want to cry in frustration. I said the damn prayer perfectly! How can they twist this around?

I'm doomed.

My knees are starting to buckle, and I grab onto the low railing in front of me to keep from fainting.

Stay alert . . . I've got to stay alert.

If I let myself lose consciousness, who knows what they'll do to me? I might never wake up again.

Finally, the judge restores order and addresses the courtroom. "The prisoner was able to recite the Lord's Prayer only through the intervention of the devil," he announces, as though that's a perfectly reasonable assumption. "This, alone, is evidence enough to convict her. However, I shall request further verification of her guilt."

What now?

The magistrate turns to me. "The prisoner shall reveal the talisman she wears around her neck."

I stare at him, unmoving. Do they actually expect my medallion to prove—

"Reveal the talisman!" he commands again.

"No!" I shout right back at him.

Then I do something really impulsive—and really stupid.

Even though I know I have no chance, I take one anyway, because all I can think is that I have to escape.

I try to run.

But I've forgotten about the shackles and chains around my ankles. The moment I move, I lose my balance and fall.

Again there's an uproar in the courtroom. Ezekiel Browne and the short jailor are grabbing me beneath my arms and yanking me painfully to my feet.

Then Ezekiel Browne reaches forward and grabs for the chain around my neck. "Here!" he hollers, and the courtroom immediately quiets down. " 'Tis here, the talisman she wears as evidence of her witchery."

He's nearly strangling me as he holds the Beatles medallion up for everyone to see.

Once again, the idiot jurors and spectators gasp and shy away.

"Touch that not, Goodman Browne!" the magistrate warns. " 'Tis an object of the devil. It may possess the power to bewitch thee."

"Yeah, Goodman Browne," I can't help taunting. "You might end up bewitched, too. Better watch out—maybe it's already happened."

He gasps, drops my silver chain and steps backward, staring at me in dread.

The next thing I know, his eyes are bulging and he's clutching his throat. Then he flings himself to the floor, kicking his legs and making hideous choking noises.

"He is bewitched!" the magistrate yells frantically.

The judge stands up and gestures toward two men standing against the wall. "Goodman Winthrop, Goodman Richardson—remove the victim from the courtroom!"

Two men reluctantly come forward and drag the ranting Ezekiel down the aisle and out the door as everyone in the room—including me—gapes in horror. The door bangs shut behind them, and an excited buzz goes up.

"Order! Order!" The judge bangs on his wooden stand.

Gradually, the hubbub dies down and the magistrate starts speaking again. "Never in the history of Seacliffe has an accused person come to trial within twenty-four hours, nor has a trial lasted only a single day. But the prisoner poses a deadly threat to the good people of Seacliffe. Under these terrifying circumstances, I would ask that this—outsider—be convicted as swiftly as possible so that we can drive her evil powers from our midst."

"That isn't fair!" I burst out. "This isn't how it's done— you have to hear *my* side. You can't just convict me on the basis of—"

"Very well. What dost thou wish to confess to the court?"

"I don't wish to 'confess' anything," I say incredulously. "I'm innocent."

"If thou art indeed innocent, then what explanation can thou offer for the bewitching of poor, afflicted Ezekiel Crane? And for the evidence presented by the Goodwife Crane that the devil visited this courtroom on thy behalf?"

"I don't know why Ezekiel Crane went crazy! Maybe he has epilepsy," I add, suddenly remembering Josie's little brother Mickey, who has epileptic fits.

The judge, magistrate, and jurors are just staring at me like they've never heard of the disease.

"And the Goodwife Crane is obviously seeing things."

Instantly, voices pipe up among the spectators, protesting that they, too, saw the devil.

The magistrate turns angrily to me. "Goody Crane is a respected member of the community of Seacliffe," he informs me. "How dare thee accuse her of seeing things?"

It's no use. These people are going to condemn me no matter what I say or do.

I don't know why I'm trying to stop them. I already know what's going to happen to me.

I think about the strands of silky red hair poking out from under the blanket.

You can't change history.

"Dost thou have any other words to speak in thy behalf, prisoner?" asks the judge, like he just wants to be fair.

I narrow my eyes at him and refuse to answer.

"Because the prisoner is a threat to the people of Seacliffe, and because she hath steadfastly refused to cooperate with this court, I beg of the jury that a decision be reached before sundown."

I can't believe what I'm hearing. This is unreal.

It's so easy to believe that this is just a terrible nightmare that I don't even feel any real panic.

I squeeze my eyes shut and pray.

Any moment now, I'm going to wake up and find myself back in my bed in New York City in 1963.

Please . . .

I open my eyes again and see only that the jury is filing out of the room.

The door closes behind them, and the judge bangs on his stand. "The court will now adjourn while the jury deliberates these charges. I ask that—"

Suddenly, the door bangs open again, cutting him off in midsentence.

The jury is filing back in, and every one of them is staring at me with hatred in his eyes.

"Hath the jury reached a verdict so quickly?" asks the judge, like he's surprised.

A sallow-faced man steps forward. "We have."

"What say thee?"

"We the jury find the defendant guilty on all charges."

I close my eyes as a cheer goes up in the courtroom.

After a moment, I realize that they're chanting something. It's "Death to the witch! Death to the witch!"

My chest feels like it's constricting and I can't move, I can't speak. I'm paralyzed with fear.

"Order!" the judge shouts. "Under these unusual circumstances, I believe 'tis my duty to hand down a sentence immediately."

He rises and turns to face me.

"Hath thee any confession to make before I decide thy punishment?"

"No," I tell him. "I can't confess because I'm not guilty of anything. But I will tell you this. If you dare try to punish me for a crime I didn't commit, I'll make you sorry."

He has the gall to smile. "And how doth thou expect to accomplish that?"

"I'll . . . I'll . . ." I'm thinking frantically, and then I remember something.

Maybe it'll work.

I look him in the eye and say triumphantly, "If you don't set me free right this second, I'll conjure up a storm! A terrible storm—the worst this town has ever seen."

The judge stares at me for a moment, as though he's trying to decide whether to believe me.

Then he turns to the courtroom. "The people of Seacliffe have heard the prisoner's confession," he announces with a terrible grin.

"But I didn't confess to anything!" I protest.

"Only a witch would threaten to 'conjure a storm,' " he informs me. " 'Twas all I needed to hear. I will now determine thy sentence. I will ask that the penalty be carried out swiftly, before the sabbath on the day after next."

Dazed, I keep looking straight ahead, seeing nothing but

the faces of the people I love off in the distance—my parents . . . the twins . . . Josie . . .

"Prisoner," the judge says in an ominous voice, "Thou hath been convicted by this court of practicing the devil's witchcraft. I do hereby sentence thee to death by hanging at dawn tomorrow."

EIGHTEEN

I spent the rest of the day on the dirt floor of my cell, my arms chained above my head. After a few hours of sobbing miserably, I gradually calmed down. Maybe I even dozed off—my entire body is aching and exhausted.

But now I'm wide awake, listening to something scurrying in the corner of the cell. It's probably a rat.

Normally, that realization would be enough to rouse me into hysterics.

But right now, all I feel is numb.

It must be getting dark outside, because I can see candle-light flickering somewhere down the corridor. The jailor and another man are there. I can hear their voices—it sounds like they're drinking and playing cards.

I'm staring off into space and wishing this whole night-mare would end when suddenly, I hear something off in the distance, so far away that I'm not even sure it's there.

Then it grows louder—a roaring, thundering sound, like a train approaching—except that there were no trains in 1692.

I hear the men's voices rising, startled, and then suddenly they're drowned out by something that slams into the build-ing so violently that the stone walls are shaking.

It takes me a few seconds to realize that it's the wind, a high-pitched, continuous howling, and it brings rain that beats furiously against the ceiling and walls like a stampede.

The storm has arrived.

The roaring wind, booming thunder, and torrential rains have been steady for several hours now. I just lie here on the dirt floor, dully listening to the storm and wondering how I'm ever going to get through the night, knowing what's waiting for me tomorrow.

Somewhere in the back of my mind, I feel like this is so bizarre, it still isn't real. And even if it is really happening to me, I can't believe that I'm actually going to die—that there's no way out. I guess I'm thinking that somehow, I'll be able to escape.

Maybe that vague notion is the only thing that's keeping me from panic.

Or maybe it's just that I've been through so much that my emotions are shot. I can't feel anything anymore.

Every once in a while, I become half aware that something large and heavy has gone flying against one of the stone walls of the prison. I vaguely suppose that it's probably just branches, but then I hear the jailor, Benjamin, shouting that some of the houses on the commons are being destroyed, and whole trees are uprooted.

Then footsteps pound down the corridor, and I glance up to see him gripping the bars of my cell. "Thou hath unleashed the devil's fury upon us!" he accuses. "I beg thee to stop this immediately."

I look at him coldly. "Not unless you set me free."

Now the other man is beside him, and I see that it's the magistrate. "Stop this madness, Witch!" he shouts above the howling wind.

"I will if you let me go."

The two men look at each other as though they're actually considering it.

Then Benjamin says, "Those houses were constructed of wood. This prison is made of stone. The storm cannot destroy it, too. Surely we are safe here."

"I wouldn't count on it," I warn him. "If you don't set me free, you'll be sorry."

"Thy words are folly!" says the magistrate after a moment's hesitation. But he doesn't look too sure.

"Come, Thomas," says the jailor. "Let us take another sip of brandy to calm our nerves."

Thomas doesn't need to be asked twice, and the two men disappear down the corridor.

Angrily, I jerk my arms as hard as I can, hoping that somehow, I'll be able to get out of these iron cuffs. But the metal only digs sharply into my already raw wrists, and I can feel something warm and sticky trickling down my arms—blood.

Tears swim into my eyes.

And all at once, an acute rush of emotion washes over me. I'm in pain, I'm filthy, and I'm scared out of my mind.

"Please," I say aloud in desperation. My voice sounds hollow and lost in the dank cell. "I want my mommy. I want my mommy . . . please, somebody, help me . . ."

And then the tears spill over again.

Somehow, I must have fallen asleep again.

The storm is howling as powerfully as ever when I wake up.

It takes me a moment to realize that something else—a new sound—has startled me awake . . .

Footsteps coming down the corridor.

And a clanking that I suddenly recognize—it's the jailor's heavy ring of cell keys.

They're going to let me out of here after all!

I lean forward and see both men approaching the iron bars. Sure enough, the jailor is searching for the right key. He finds it and inserts it into the lock.

They must have decided they've had enough of this storm.

By the time they realize that I'm not able to control it after all, I'll be out of here—back in 1963, where they can't get me.

My mind is already racing ahead. As soon as they let me go, I'll get back to the Crane house and the secret cupboard. Then . . .

Benjamin and the magistrate step into my cell and look down at me. I notice that they look unsteady and bleary-eyed. And they reek of liquor.

"Hast thou any words to offer?" the magistrate asks me.

"Yes. Set me free, and I promise I'll stop the storm," I tell him.

"Set her free!" the magistrate repeats to the jailor, and at first I think that's an order.

Then I realize he's laughing.

My stomach turns over with a sickening thud.

"The prisoner believes we are about to set her free!" he slurs, shaking his head.

The jailor giggles, his shiny face mottled from drinking. "Set her free?" he keeps repeating. "Set her free?"

The magistrate leans over so that his face is right in front of mine. His breath is hot and stinks of alcohol. "On the contrary, Witch. We are going to carry out the execution order."

"But . . . it's not dawn! You can't—" Bile rises up into

my throat, threatening to choke me. I force the burning acid back down, make myself look him in the eye.

" 'Tis close enough to dawn," the magistrate says. "If thou will refuse to put an end to the tempest thou hast wrought, we shall put an end to thee!"

"No!" I shriek as the jailor reaches out to unlock the cuffs around my wrists.

The magistrate clumsily grabs on to me and holds me until the cuffs are off. The jailor fiddles with a piece of rope, getting ready to tie my hands together.

Suddenly, I lift my arm and jab my elbow as hard as I can into the jailor's crotch. He screams and doubles over in agony as I wrench myself out of the startled magistrate's grasp.

With a burst of adrenaline, I lunge toward the iron-barred door to the cell, which is standing ajar.

I'm almost through it when something closes around my ankle and pulls me backward.

It's the magistrate's giant hand, and then his other arm is crooked around my throat and I'm being tossed roughly to the ground.

"Do not attempt to escape," the magistrate says in a low, evil voice right next to my ear. "Tie her hands!"

The jailor is still gasping and sputtering.

"I command thee, Benjamin, tie her hands!"

Still groaning in pain, he roughly grabs the rope and pulls my arms behind me. He whips the rope around my wrists, yanking it so tightly that it digs brutally into my already raw skin.

But it's as though I'm becoming immune to the physical suffering—and again, to emotion.

I just stand there, wearily submissive, as they fasten heavy shackles and chains around my ankles.

Then I see them coming at me with a black hood. I feel

only the merest flicker of terror as it descends over my head, and then I'm alone in the suffocating blackness. The coarse fabric is pulled tightly against my face, and I can barely breathe, but it doesn't matter anymore.

Nothing matters.

I just want this to end.

"Walk!" the magistrate commands, and, with both of them gripping my upper arms, I move a few steps, dragging the chains along the ground.

"Faster!"

They propel me forward and I oblige blindly, vaguely aware that cool air is blowing toward me.

Then we're outside, and I almost lose my balance as the wind slams into me. The men shout directions at each other and pull me along. It's harder to walk now; we're moving against the wind and the chains at my ankles are getting heavier as I drag them through mud.

Rain drenches me. The hood becomes sodden and plastered against my face, and it's almost impossible for me to suck air through it. I'm gasping for each breath, becoming light-headed as we keep plodding along, the storm raging around us and drowning out their voices.

And then we're stopping, and I feel them hoisting me into the air.

I know that I should fight.

But I'm too drained.

I just don't care anymore.

Now I'm being set down on top of something, and I numbly realize what it must be.

The platform underneath the tree where they hung Felicity.

My legs start to buckle, but they're clutching my arms, holding me up.

And then everything starts happening in a faraway, slow

motion sequence as my mind fills with echoing voices and random images.

. . . my mother singing nursery rhymes to me . . . my father ruffling my hair and calling me "Abbey-my-girl" . . . the twins fighting over a red toy fire truck . . .

I'm dimly aware of something coming down over the hood and resting against my shoulders before they tighten it so that it encircles my neck.

The noose.

. . . Josie passing me a note in class . . . Josie, with her unruly, crookedly parted black hair . . . Katie, with that blond ponytail . . .

"Would thee wish to confess thy crimes now, before being sent to thy doom?" the magistrate bellows over the swirling storm.

. . . Riley Kennedy opening a door for me, saying, "After you, New Yo-awk" . . .

"Hast thou any last words?"

. . . "Please, Abbey . . . get back to my Zachariah somehow . . . my dying thoughts shall be of him" . . .

"She speaketh not! 'Tis time to carry out the execution."

. . . Felicity's bright blue eyes, begging me . . .

"Thomas, help me to move the platform away."

. . . Zachariah's voice . . .

"Now, witch, we send thee to thy eternal damnation!"

. . . Zachariah, shouting something . . .

There's a lurch beneath my feet, and then suddenly, I'm falling.

NINETEEN

"No!"

It's an agonized scream, rising above the fury of the storm, filling my ears as I plummet . . .

And I realize it's coming from Zachariah—how can he be here?—just as my feet hit something that abruptly stops their descent.

Someone has caught me; strong arms are holding my legs so that I won't drop any further and the noose won't tighten around my neck.

Then I'm swiftly being shoved upward, and my feet are touching the platform again.

"Stand," he commands hurriedly in a hoarse voice from somewhere below. "Stand, or the rope will tighten and strangle thee."

I obey automatically, forcing my rubbery legs to hold me up.

Nearby, the jailor is cut off abruptly in the middle of a shout, and I can hear a scuffle that ends with a groan and a thud.

Then the platform is shaking violently as someone climbs onto it, and I almost lose my balance and pitch forward off the edge.

But Zachariah catches me, wrapping his arms around me from behind, holding me close against his solid chest.

Despite the incessant blowing wind, I can clearly hear his voice, low and tender in my hood-covered ear, saying, "Oh, my love, how I have longed to be near thee. Hold steady, now, just another moment . . ."

He lets go, but I can feel him behind me, sawing frantically at the rope tied to the branch above.

I focus every ounce of energy I have left into keeping my balance, allowing myself to think of nothing but the fact that I must not fall.

Then the rope gives way, and the noose is being loosened and yanked up and over my hood.

Suddenly, I'm overtaken by a violent trembling, I feel myself swaying . . .

"No, Felicity!" Again, I'm wrapped in those powerful arms. He squeezes me briefly, then lowers me so that I'm lying on the platform.

The cold rain beats a soothing rhythm over my body as I fade away, floating toward a peaceful, quiet darkness . . .

His words are coming from far off, barely audible. "We must hurry away, my love, before they awaken . . ." Now he's sobbing and clutching me to him, whispering Felicity's name over and over.

I listen helplessly, trying to respond, to tell him that he's mistaken—that I'm not Felicity.

I have to tell him—I struggle against the blackness, but I'm gradually losing the strength to keep it away.

"Oh, Felicity," Zachariah is saying, "I am so thankful that I arrived in time. I could not bear to live without thee."

I vaguely realize that he's tugging at the hood that's covering my head. I feel it moving upward, then becoming tangled in my hair.

"Be patient, my darling . . ."

Then he gently pulls it free.

Even over the noise of the storm I can hear his horrified gasp. "Abigail!"

I turn my head slightly, tilting my face upward so that the cool, clean rain streams over my skin.

And just before I lose consciousness, I feel myself being lifted and carried away.

I wake up again to an eerie silence.

Startled, I open my eyes and see nothing but blackness all around. Then I realize that it's still night, and I'm lying on the marshy ground in the woods.

The storm is over.

"Abigail?"

I turn my head toward the sound of Zachariah's voice. He's sitting beside me, silhouetted against the dark sky.

"Zachariah," I try to say, but my voice comes out a mere croak. I force it out. "Where are we?"

"In a clearing off the trail. We are headed back to the Crane house, but I grew too exhausted to go any further without a rest." He reaches over and rests a hand against my cheek. "Abigail, how did thee come to be here, in 1692?"

I just shake my head mutely, unable to muster the strength to speak again.

"Abigail," he says slowly, "I must know. My Felicity, is she—did I arrive too late to save her?"

I hesitate, then nod and close my eyes again.

"Oh, no . . . no!" Anguished sobs fill the quiet night air.

I gather my strength, reach out blindly and find his hand. I squeeze it tightly and he clings to me, and after a while he stops crying.

Then he says, "We must move on again, before daylight."

"Where . . ." I test my voice, and find that it works.

"Where are the men who were trying to kill me? What happened to them?"

"I caught them unaware," he says quietly. "I was able to hit them from behind and knock them down just as they began pulling the platform from beneath your feet. The taller man—I believe he was Thomas Darwin, the magistrate, fell unconscious into the mud. But the other man gave me a bit more trouble, and I was forced to seize a nearby tree limb and hit him with it."

"But where did you come from, Zachariah?" I ask, dragging my leaden body into a sitting position. He reaches over to help me. "How did you get here?"

"I believed that Felicity was there, in 1963, and that she would find me," he says slowly. "But in the night, as I lay sleeping in the tall grass near the water, I heard someone calling my name. I did not recognize the voice, and when I peered out, I saw that 'twas Elspeth Andrewes. I was so stunned to see her that I could not speak until after she had passed. And that was when I realized that 'twas Elspeth, and not Felicity, who had traveled to 1963. That meant Elspeth was up to something—I have never trusted her. And—"

"Zachariah, she's the person whose name I couldn't remember," I break in to tell him. "She was the one who accused Felicity of witchcraft. She's in love with you, Zachariah. She hated Felicity. She was trying to get her out of the way."

"I shall make her pay," he says, his voice tight with hatred. "Somehow, she will pay."

"What happened next, Zachariah?"

"I knew Felicity was still in danger. I was desperate to get back to 1692 and rescue her . . ." He pauses and shakes his head, unable to go on.

It takes him a long time to regain his composure. Finally,

he clears his throat and continues, "I stole through the woods under cover of darkness. In the undergrowth behind thy dwelling, I found the herbs I needed. I brought them back to my camp and dried them early that morning in the heat of the fire."

I listen as he describes how he spent the day hiding from Elspeth and making his plans. When night fell again, he slipped back through the woods and quietly got into the house through a loose screen in a first-floor window. He hurried to the secret cupboard, and in a matter of minutes, he had returned to 1692. There was no sign of the Cranes when he emerged from the cupboard.

He found that the terrible storm was raging outside, but he knew he couldn't stay in the house and let them find him. So he struggled against the wind and rain and pushed his way along the trail toward town. When he got there, he saw the two men marching a hooded prisoner toward the make-shift gallows on the commons. He hid nearby, then snuck up and knocked them out just in time.

It wasn't hard to fight them both, he adds ruefully, because they were staggering drunk.

When he's finished with his story, I tell him mine.

As soon as I tell him that Elspeth tried to kill me, he clenches his fists and bursts out, "I shall see that she is punished."

I nod and go on, recounting everything that happened to me. I reach the part about Felicity, and it's hard, but I tell him everything.

"She said that her last words would be of you, Zachariah," I finish, and tears are streaming down my face. "She was so brave . . . even when they were taking her away."

He's sobbing again, too.

Finally, we pull ourselves together. "We must return to

the secret cupboard before dawn, while they are still asleep upstairs," Zachariah says abruptly. "Soon it will be light, and it will be too late. I shall carry you—"

"No! I can walk now."

He looks dubious, but I start to get up and he hurriedly springs forward and helps me to my feet.

I take a few unsteady steps, testing my legs. They're wobbly, and I ache all over.

"Let me carry you, Abigail."

"Uh-uh," I say firmly. "I can make it. Let's go."

And together, we set off through the woods again.

No one is stirring and the windows are all dark as we approach the familiar house nearly an hour later.

"Good . . . they are still asleep," Zachariah whispers to me. "We have time."

But the sky in the east is milky and growing dangerously brighter, and I know we have no time to waste. He grabs my hand and pulls me forward, across the overgrown field that will someday be a backyard. I have no time to marvel at the differences between the shabby, unpainted house in 1692 and how it looks today—or rather, tomorrow.

Zachariah puts a finger up against his lips, motioning me to be quiet as he turns the knob on the back door and opens it.

I frown. "There's no lock?" I whisper.

He just shakes his head and steps quietly inside. I follow him.

We creep through the shadowy kitchen, which looks oddly bare without the stove, refrigerator, sink, and cupboards. Even though it's dark, I can see that all that remains the same is the low ceiling with its exposed beams, and the giant brick fireplace that's big enough to stand in—except they really use it for cooking, and there are big iron pots and skillets hanging everywhere.

I only have time to give the room a quick glance before Zachariah propels me forward, through the passageway to the keeping room.

He opens the door to the cupboard, then carefully feels around for the secret lever. I hear a quiet click as the secret door opens, and then he reaches into his pocket and pulls something out. It's a cluster of dried leaves.

He places them into my palm, then gestures for me to get inside the closet.

I widen my eyes at him. "You're coming, too, Zachariah, aren't you?" I ask softly.

He shakes his head. "I do not belong there."

"But you can't stay here!" I whisper frantically. "They'll kill you if they find you. And without Felicity—" I break off, watching his face.

After a moment, he nods. "I will go back," he says, "but only for a short time. Only until I find Elspeth Andrewes and make her pay." Though his voice is hushed, I can hear the pure hatred when he mentions her name.

"And then where will you go?"

"I do not know. Perhaps—"

Just then, a rooster crows somewhere outside.

"Come—hurry!" Zachariah grabs my arm and shoves me inside the inner cupboard. He pulls the outer door shut, then steps in beside me and closes the inner door. It's so cramped with the two of us here that I'm jammed up against the wall with him right against me.

"All right, Abigail. . . . Concentrate," he hisses in the darkness.

I close my eyes and think about home. I want so badly to

be back in my own time again that a lump rises in my throat and I can barely get around it to speak.

I gulp and join Zachariah, methodically repeating "1963," careful not to let my tongue become twisted.

I think about my parents, and the twins, and Riley—

A tingling current suddenly zaps through me.

"Zachariah?" I whisper tentatively. "Did you feel that?"

"Yes," he says quietly.

I feel him lifting his arm, and then there's a clicking sound as the door springs open. Zachariah steps forward and I take a deep breath and cross my fingers.

I hear him feeling for the knob on the second door.

And then it's opening with a faint creak and a shaft of dim light filters in.

Zachariah steps out into the keeping room, then turns back to me with a little smile. "Come along, Abigail," he whispers. " 'Tis 1963."

TWENTY

We're just standing here in the shadowy keeping room, Zachariah and I, and I'm so happy to be back—Elspeth or no Elspeth—that I could kiss this scarred old wooden floor. I can hear my father snoring upstairs, and there, on the hearth of the fireplace, is a rubberbanded stack of the twins' Yankee baseball cards.

I turn to Zachariah, about to thank him again. But my smile fades when I see his expression.

His eyes, still tear-stained and puffy from crying, are filled with despair.

"Oh, Zachariah," I murmur, reaching out to touch his shoulder.

He just shakes his head sadly. "If only I had been able to get there in time," he whispers. "If only I could have saved her."

There's nothing I can say to that. I just stroke the coarse, still damp fabric of his sleeve and stare at the floor.

And then suddenly it dawns on me—an idea so simple, so brilliant, that I can't believe we both overlooked it.

"Zachariah!" I burst out urgently, and he automatically lifts a finger against his lips, shushing me. I'm so excited that I can barely lower my voice. "Why didn't we think of this before? There *is* a way for you to go back and save Felicity!"

"How?" he demands, careful to keep his voice hushed.

"You can go back to today's date in 169*1!*" I announce in a triumphant stage whisper. "A whole year before Felicity was accused of witchcraft. All you have to do is change the course of events that lead up to Felicity's execution."

He looks doubtful, but I can see a flicker of excitement in his eyes. "How would I be able to do that?"

"I don't know—warn her about Elspeth. Stop her from fooling around with Jemima's magic spells and charms. Do whatever you have to do—it can't be that difficult," I say impatiently. I'm still annoyed with myself—and him—for not having thought of this sooner. But I guess we were both too preoccupied to think beyond just getting out of there.

Zachariah still doesn't seem convinced. "Can it be possible to alter the events of history?"

I ponder that for a moment, then I slap my forehead in sudden realization. "Of course it's possible. You saved me, didn't you? And I was in all the history books as the mysterious second witch who was executed. I'll bet that if we look in a history book right now, we'll see that it's changed."

He's shaking his head in wonder. "I cannot believe that there may still be a chance that I will save Felicity . . ."

"Zachariah, not only is there a chance, there's a way. Now stop wasting time and get back there to her." And I gesture toward the cupboard.

He's already hurrying toward it, fumbling in his pocket. He produces another cluster of the herbs, then breaks off a sprig and offers it to me. "Take this. In case thou would ever care to return and visit Felicity and me."

I just wave it away. "I don't think so," I tell him. "No offense, but I'm not very anxious to go back to the seventeenth century anytime soon."

"Then we shall never see each other again, Abigail?" He pauses, one hand on the closet doorknob, looking at me.

"I don't think so." A pang of sadness darts through me and I feel a little lump rising in my throat. "I'm going to miss you," I say in a small voice.

"I shall never forget thee, Abigail. Some day, I vow, I will find a way to thank thee."

We're standing there, looking wistfully at each other, when suddenly, a floorboard creaks overhead.

"Someone's up!" I whisper frantically. "Go!"

I shove him into the closet and close the door after him, and I hear his muffled voice calling, "God keep thee, dear Abigail."

Then there's a barely audible click from behind the door, and I know he's opened the secret cupboard.

Now I hear footsteps walking down the stairs. They're too light to belong to either of my parents. It must be one of the twins—they're usually up at the crack of dawn, which is exactly what this is. Dim morning light is filtering through the windows along the east wall.

Belatedly, I glance down and realize I'm still wearing this filthy rag of a dress over my clothes. In one frantic movement, I yank it up over my head and shove it behind a sofa just as Peter comes padding into the keeping room in his pajamas and slippers. He stops, wide-eyed, when he sees me.

"Abbey?"

"Petey!" I'm completely overwhelmed by the sight of his familiar, freckled little face. I rush forward and throw my arms around him, kissing his stubbly hair.

"Abbey, you smell funny. And why are you all wet? Where were you?"

"Uh . . . where do you think I was?" I ask cautiously, pulling back and looking at him.

"Back in New York. Mom and Dad said you ran away. They said you probably took a bus home. They called Josie and everyone and said you were probably on your way there. And they called the police, and Mommy keeps crying, and I cried, and even Paul did, too! And Daddy is upset, 'cause he says you left on account of how you were mad at him. Did you?"

"Yes, I did," I say, promptly latching on to his explanation. It makes perfect sense, even though I hate to keep lying to everyone. "But then I changed my mind before I got to New York, and I decided to come back here because I missed everyone."

At least that's the truth—well, the last part, anyway.

"I'm glad . . . even though you kind of stink," he says honestly, wrinkling his freckled little nose.

I step back from him. "I've got to go upstairs and take a bath right away, before anyone else wakes up. Don't tell Mom and Dad I'm home until I get out of the bathroom, okay?"

"Okay. I'll go have some cereal," he says, yawning, and goes shuffling off.

As soon as I hear him in the kitchen, dragging a chair over to reach a cupboard, I hurry over to the closet beside the fireplace. I open the door, then release the latch for the secret cupboard.

I know it's empty even before I peek inside.

But there, on the floor, I can see a clump of dried herbs Zachariah left there for me.

I quickly shut the door, leaving them there.

I didn't even get to say a real goodbye, I think regretfully as I hurry into the hall. But I'm glad he's gone back. I just know he'll manage to save Felicity.

I'm halfway up the stairs when I remember something.

Something that sends a finger of cold fear to squeeze my heart.

Elspeth.

* * *

I'm just stepping out of the tub when someone knocks on the bathroom door.

"Peter? Is that you in there?"

It's my father's gruff, early morning voice.

I don't answer, just grab a towel and start drying off.

He knocks again, louder. "Peter? Come on, I've got to get in there."

I pull on the nightgown I'd grabbed from my room, then wrap the towel, turban-style, around my head.

"No, Dad," I announce, finally opening the door. "It's me."

He just stares in disbelief. Then he throws his arms around me and squeezes me so tightly I'm in instant pain. My entire body still feels battered and bruised from my ordeal.

"Thank God you're all right," my father is saying into my hair in a ragged tone I've never heard before.

And I think, *Good—he's so happy to see me that I'm not going to get into trouble.*

Wrong.

The next thing out of his mouth, as soon as he lets go of me, is, "How the hell could you take off like that? Do you know what your mother and I have been through for the past day and a half? Do you?"

"No," I say in a small voice.

"Frank? What's going on?" My mother comes running out into the hall and bursts into tears when she catches sight of me. "Abbey!" she cries, and rushes toward me.

I wince and brace myself for another excruciating embrace.

The second my mother's done hugging me, she steps back with her hands on her hips, her eyes still wet and shiny, and demands, "Where have you been, young lady?"

"I . . . I started to go home to New York because I hated

it here so much," I say, hoping it doesn't sound too rehearsed. "But then I changed my mind, because I knew how worried you'd be—" I throw that in for good measure. "So I got off the bus, and it took a while until I could catch one heading back here."

"Oh, Abbey, how could you run away like that?" My mother shakes her head at me. "If I weren't so glad to see you safe and sound, I'd . . ." She just shakes her head again.

"I'm really sorry." I start to cry. "I don't know what happened. I didn't mean to upset everyone . . ."

"Well, Abigail, at least you had the sense to turn around and come back." My father still looks mad, but he reaches out and squeezes my aching arm.

I try not to flinch. Sniffling, I say truthfully, "All I wanted was to come home to you and Mom."

Down the hall, Paul's door opens and he pokes his stubbly blond head out. "Is that Abbey?"

"It sure is, honey," my mom tells him.

"Hey, Abbey, guess what?" He's still rubbing sleep from his eyes.

"What?"

"Mom and Dad called the cops to tell them you were gone! And they came over here, and one of them, Officer Hanley, let me touch his badge and everything! And they let me sit in the backseat of their car—you know, where they put the bad guys. And Officer Hanley showed me how you turn on the siren, and then he—"

"Okay, Paul, that's enough. You can tell Abbey all about it later," my father interrupts. "Right now, I think she wants to go get dressed."

"Uh, actually, Dad," I say around a huge yawn, "I'm kind of tired. I haven't slept very much in the last day or two. Can I go to bed for a while?"

He and my mother exchange a glance. Then my mother shrugs and says, "All right, Abbey, go to sleep. You look like you need it. We'll talk again later, when you get up."

"Thanks." I pause. "Am I still grounded?"

I expect my father to say yes, but he doesn't. He just goes, "Maybe I was a little harsh. We'll talk about it."

"Okay." Suddenly, I'm so wiped out that I don't know if I can make it all the way to my room down the hall.

But I force my leaden legs to start moving toward it, and at last, I'm climbing under the covers and letting my head sink into the welcoming pillow.

My last thought before I slip effortlessly into a heavy sleep is that with any luck, I'll be too exhausted for nightmares.

"Abbey? Abbey, wake up . . . Abbey . . ."

The voice is far off, soothing, and I smile.

"Abbey!"

That time it's louder, jerking me out of the dreamy, peaceful place.

I open my eyes and see my mother standing over me. "Abbey, it's almost noon."

"Mmm-hmm." I roll over groggily and start to drift again.

"Abigail Harmon, it's time to wake up. Now, come on. You have a visitor."

I roll back again and look at her. "Who is it?" I murmur.

"It's Katie Kennedy."

Déjà vu. "Tell her I'll be down later."

"No. It's nearly afternoon. You can't sleep the day away. I'll give you fifteen minutes to get downstairs." She turns and walks toward the door, calling over her shoulder, "I mean it. Fifteen minutes, Abbey."

I sigh and try to collect my scattered thoughts.

Katie.

It seems like years have gone by since I last saw her.

Groaning in pain, I get up out of bed and walk across the room to the mirror above my dresser.

What I see there yanks the last bit of drowsiness right out of me.

I look hideous. My hair has dried into a big puffy, tangled mess, but it goes beyond that. My face is drawn and pale and there are enormous dark trenches under my eyes. I look like I've been through a war.

And it's going to take longer than fifteen minutes to repair the damage.

There's nothing to do but grab my hairbrush and begin.

"Katie?" Coming into the kitchen, I see her sitting at the table.

"Abbey! Hi!" She stands up and flashes a somewhat dimmer version of her Katie-grin.

"Hi." I look around. "Where is everyone? Did my parents go someplace?"

"Uh-huh. They just left. They said to tell you they had to go see Ted Leeworthy. They'll be back in an hour or two."

"Who?"

"Ted Leeworthy. They said you'd know. I think he's the contractor or something."

I shrug. "I'm terrible with names," I tell her, just for something to say. I notice that she's nervously fumbling with the pockets on her peach-colored sundress.

"Abbey," she says tentatively, looking up at me. "I feel really bad about everything that happened."

"About what?" I ask carefully, walking over to the table

and sitting down. I'm still too wobbly to stand for any amount of time without feeling like I'm going to keel over.

"About, you know, everything." She plops back into her chair and starts talking in a rush. "I mean, when I saw Peter on the driveway this morning and he told me you were back home, I was so relieved, because when I heard you had run away, I felt so guilty about the way I treated you the other day, the day you told me about you and Riley. It's just that I'm so used to girls who only want to be my friend so that they can hang around him, and I thought you were different, but then . . ." She trails off and sits there looking at her hands twisting anxiously in her lap.

"It's okay, Katie," I say.

Suddenly I'm overcome by guilt, myself, about the way I treated her. I mean, she really is sweet, and she was trying so hard to be my friend. And all I did was mope around wishing she were Josie and being irritated by her bubbly, enthusiastic personality.

"It must be hard having a brother like Riley," I tell her after a pause. "I understand how you felt."

"You do?" She looks relieved. "Honestly?"

"Sure. You know, I'm starving," I add quickly—mostly because it's true, but also because I don't want to get into anything mushy with Katie, who looks dangerously poised to throw her arms around me.

I unbend my stiff limbs and stand up, trying not to wince. "Are you hungry?"

"Not really, but go ahead."

I try to walk casually across the kitchen to the cupboards, but every step is excruciating.

"Abbey, are you all right?" Katie asks immediately.

"Sure, I'm fine." But when I gingerly reach up to open

the cupboard, a fierce dagger of pain shoots through my shoulder and I can't help crying out, "Ow!"

"Abbey, what's wrong? Did you hurt yourself?" Katie's across the kitchen in a few quick steps and standing at my side, looking concerned.

I stare at her, debating.

And then I go, impulsively, "Listen, Katie, can you keep a secret?"

"Of course!" she says, her cheeks instantly becoming flushed with excitement.

I watch her warily, wondering if I'm about to make a big mistake. Then I decide that I don't care if I am. I'm sick of lying. Suddenly, I feel the acute need to tell somebody the whole story, and Katie is one of the few people who probably won't think I'm crazy.

"Okay," I say after another moment, "I'm going to tell you what really happened . . ." My stomach growls loudly then, and I add, "But first—would you mind fixing me a bowl of cereal?"

TWENTY-ONE

"I can't believe it," Katie says, shaking her head and staring at me with round green eyes. "I mean . . . I can't believe it!"

"C'mon, Katie, you've said that about a million times now. Don't you have anything else to say?"

She shrugs. "It's just so . . . unbelievable."

I chime in with her on that last word, then give her a pointed look. "Katie!"

"All right, all right . . . but what do you want me to say?" She shivers. "It's so creepy. I mean, this Elspeth person is just lurking around here now. She's dangerous. Maybe you should go to the police."

"And tell them what?"

She hesitates. "I see what you mean. But aren't you scared? I mean, what if she comes after you again?"

"She won't," I say, feigning a casual, bland attitude.

"How do you know?"

"I . . ." Let's face it, this is ridiculous. I *am* scared—in fact, I'm terrified. Why deny it? "I don't know," I admit to Katie. "I'm just hoping."

We stare at each other. The worried expression on Katie's face is getting to me, so I say abruptly, "Come on, let's change the subject now."

"Okay. So, when can we try this time travel thing?"

"Katie, are you out of your mind?"

"Calm down, Abbey—of course I'm not out of my mind. Can't you see the possibilities?"

"No." I stand up stiffly and carry my empty cereal bowl over to the sink.

"Abbey—"

"No." I turn on the water and rinse out the bowl. "I refuse to go back in time ever again. It's too dangerous."

"So? Who cares about going *back* in time, anyway? I mean, it would be fun to see what things were like, but we basically already know, anyway. I'm talking about going *forward*."

I stop and ponder the idea.

Going forward?

Now *that* would be interesting.

"Wouldn't it be fun to see what things are going to be like in the future?" Katie asks.

"We could find out if JFK gets that man on the moon or not . . ." I say slowly. "And whether the Beatles will ever become popular in America. That would be great—then I wouldn't have to wait for Siobhan to send me their newest records. I could buy them myself—or hear them on the radio!"

"Yeah, but, Abbey, think of what else you could find out. I mean, on a more personal level."

"Like what?"

"Who you're going to marry, for one thing!"

I frown. "I don't really care about that," I tell her. But I wouldn't mind seeing what Riley will look like in about ten years . . .

"Well, there are other things you can find out, then," Katie says hastily. "Come on, Abbey, let's go try it. You said Zachariah left you a bunch of herbs."

"Not that many."

"So? We'll pick more. They grow behind your house, right? It can't be that hard to figure out which ones they are." Katie pushes her chair back and starts walking toward the keeping room. "Come on," she calls back over her shoulder. "Let's try it now, before your parents get back."

"I don't know, Katie . . ."

But I follow her in there, lured by the thought of seeing what Riley's going to be up to in the future.

Katie opens the closet door and peers inside. "It's dark in here. You'd never know there was a hidden cupboard in back. Where's the secret lever?"

"Here," I say, pulling her out so that I can step in. "Let me find it." I reach up and within a few seconds, the back wall has sprung open.

I hesitate, staring at it.

"What's wrong, Abbey?"

"I don't know. Maybe this isn't such a good idea. Maybe—"

"Abbey, I understand why you're a little hesitant, but don't worry. What can happen if we just go ahead a few years? We'll only stay a few minutes . . ."

"Katie, I don't know . . ."

"Oh, come on, Abbey. It'll be so much fun. Just think, we have access to something no one else in the world can know. How can we not do this? We owe it to the world, Abbey," she says dramatically. "I mean, we might find out information that can change the course of the future. We might—"

"Oh, for Pete's sake, Katie," I snap, yanking the secret door all the way open. "Come on. Let's go."

She squeals and jumps into the closet, nearly knocking me off balance as I'm reaching down for the dried bunch of herbs. I break off a few of the brittle leaves and crumble them on the floor, then carefully put the remaining sprig into the front pocket of my shorts.

"Okay," I tell Katie, "shut that door and get into the cupboard with me. It's going to be a tight fit."

"That's all right." She closes the door behind her and we're plunged into darkness.

Katie's cheerful voice asks, "How far ahead do you want to go?"

I hesitate. "Ten years?"

"Okay. 1973. I'm so nervous I feel like I'm going to wet my pants," she says as she squeezes into the cupboard next to me.

"Katie!"

"Don't worry, I won't."

"You'd better not." I close the inner door, fighting back a feeling of uneasiness.

"Now what?" Katie asks.

"Now we concentrate as hard as we can and say 1973 over and over again until it works."

"Okay."

"Ready?"

"Yes."

I close my eyes and concentrate on the future. Together, Katie and I start chanting carefully.

"1973 . . . 1973 . . . 1973 . . ."

After a few minutes, nothing has happened.

Katie breaks off the chant to whisper, "Did it work yet?"

"No."

"How do you know?"

"I don't feel anything."

"Well, maybe it worked and you just didn't realize it."

"I don't think so," I say flatly. "I'd know. I'd feel this tingling, and . . . I'd just know."

"Well, let's open the door and check anyway."

I don't argue. I'm starting to get claustrophobic, and I still can't help feeling anxious at the thought of fooling around with this time travel stuff again.

I reach up and release the latch for the inner door, then

step out into the closet and warily shove the next door open. I'm afraid of what I might see—my mother standing there in a futuristic jumpsuit and space helmet?

But everything looks exactly the same.

Just to be sure, I take a few steps out and pick up the copy of *Life* magazine that's lying on a table. There's a picture of the Vatican on the cover and the headline, *Great Princes of the Church: Among Them, the Next Pope.* That's a good sign, since Pope John the twenty-third just died a few weeks ago. I look for the date. There it is—June fourteenth, 1963.

"It didn't work," I turn around and tell Katie, relieved.

She looks disappointed. "Why not?"

"How am I supposed to know? Maybe you can't travel forward—only backward."

"That can't be right. Zachariah came forward. And so did you."

She has a point.

I frown. "Well, I don't know why it didn't work, Katie, but let's just—"

"Let's try it again. We'll pick a different year. 1972."

"I don't see how—"

"Come on, Abbey . . . please?"

After a moment, I shrug. "Okay."

We get back into the closet and do the whole routine again. It doesn't work.

Katie insists that we keep trying, so we make our way backward year by year, until we reach 1964.

Finally, we step out of the closet and I say, "Katie, I don't know what's going on, but this just isn't working."

"Maybe it never did," she says pointedly, looking me in the eye.

"What's that supposed to mean?"

"Maybe you never really went back after all, Abbey. And maybe Zachariah never—"

"Are you calling me a liar?" I cut in angrily. "Because if you are, I—"

"No! I'm not calling you a liar," she says quickly. "All I'm saying is that you've been under a lot of pressure, and maybe you just . . ."

"Imagined it?" I say evenly. "Is that it?"

"Well . . . yeah."

"You want me to prove it to you, Katie? You want to travel through time?" I step back into the secret cupboard and pull her arm. "Come on. Let's go back."

"But I thought you were afraid to travel backward."

"We'll only go back one year. 1962. Now come on."

She allows me to pull her into the cupboard and close the door. Once again we concentrate.

"1962 . . . 1962 . . . 1962 . . ."

And then it happens.

That familiar head-to-toe tingling.

I hear Katie gasp and I know she felt it too.

Then it's over—the electricity is gone.

"Did it work?" Katie's small voice asks in the dark.

"I think so. Come on."

My heart is pounding as I open the first door, then carefully push the outer door open a crack.

The *Life* magazine is gone. The room is shadowy, and I notice that the drapes are drawn against the sunlight. There's a stale, musty smell in the air.

"Did it work?" Katie asks again, her voice lowered to a whisper.

"Yes." I move forward, but she reaches out and clutches my sleeve, trying to pull me back.

"I'm afraid, Abbey."

"You're the one who wanted to do this in the first place. Now come on." I drag her with me, and we step out into the keeping room.

The house is silent.

"I wonder where Great-Uncle William is," I whisper, looking around. Everything looks pretty much the same as it did the night we moved in.

"Shhh . . . did you hear that?" Katie asks, frozen in front of the closet door.

"What?" I listen.

Someone's snoring. It sounds like it's coming from upstairs.

"It must be your uncle," Katie says, her eyes wide. "Let's get out of here."

"Don't you want to see any more?"

"No. Let's go."

"All right, if you're positive."

Before we can move, we hear something else.

Voices.

They're coming in through the window.

And they sound familiar.

"That's Riley!" Katie says in a high-pitched, startled tone.

I nod and reach over to peek through the curtain at the window. The driveway next door seems empty at first. Then I see him—Riley. Except he's several inches shorter and his hair is a little longer than it is now, cut in a Princeton style.

What I see next is so weird that it makes me turn around and stare at Katie, who's poised in the doorway of the closet.

"What? What's happening?" she asks fearfully.

I don't answer—just point out the window, gaping.

Katie comes over and peers over my shoulder.

I hear her gasp, then she grabs on to me for support.

"Abbey . . ." she says in a small voice.

I look back at her. She's pale and looks unsteady.

Then I glance back out the window.

There she is again.

And this Katie is swatting Riley in the arm, trying to convince him to do something. Her voice comes floating in the window.

"Come on, Riley . . . please? Can't I come, too?"

"Uh-uh," he says, shaking his head and grinning. "This is a date, Katie, not a group outing."

"Riley, come on . . ."

"Sorry, squirt. Sherry and I want to be alone."

I turn around and say to Katie, "Sherry?"

"His old girlfriend. He dumped her on the fourth of July last year. I remember this—he's taking her to this carnival up the coast . . ."

Outside, the other Katie has gone storming into the house, calling, "I'm telling Mom."

Riley shrugs, then walks over to the car and gets in. As he starts up the engine, I hear Katie say behind me, "Abbey, can we get out of here, please? I don't feel very good."

"Okay." We hurry back to the secret cupboard, and I sprinkle more dried leaves onto the floor before we start chanting, "1963."

It only takes a few minutes before we're stepping back out into the future—rather, the present.

Katie sinks into the nearest chair and says weakly, "That was so strange, Abbey."

"No kidding. Now do you believe me?"

"Yes."

"Good." I frown. "I wonder why it didn't work when we tried to go forward, though."

"Who knows? Who cares? You were right. It's better not to fool around with this time travel stuff."

"I agree." But I can't help wondering what's going on. There has to be a good reason why we couldn't visit the future . . .

"Abbey?"

"Hmmm?"

"You never played that record for me. You know, by that new group—what was it? The Ladybugs?"

"The Beatles," I correct her.

"Well, why don't you get your record and we'll go to my house?"

"Good idea." I give the secret cupboard one last look, then grab the record and follow Katie next door.

I'm lying in bed, trying to fall asleep.

But my mind is spinning with everything that's happened today.

First there was that whole business where Katie and I tried to travel forward, and ended up going back to last year. Then we went over to the Kennedys' and I played "Love Me Do" for her. She really liked it after we'd heard it a few times.

I showed her a picture of the Beatles, too. She immediately told me that she thinks Ringo is all right, but Paul is the best-looking one—which figures, because everybody likes Paul and I'm quickly figuring out that Katie's not the type to stray from the norm. But that's all right—I still like her. She may not be Josie, but she might end up being a good friend, anyway.

When I was getting ready to go home, Riley came back from his lifeguard job. He looked surprised and happy to see me, and Katie didn't seem to mind that he walked me back next door.

"I missed you, New Yo-*awk*," he said before I went inside. "What are you doing tomorrow night?"

"Nothing much. Why?"

"Want to go out?"

I was about to say yes when I remembered that I'm probably still grounded. "Can I let you know tomorrow? I'll have to talk to my parents."

"Sure." And he flashed that grin and gave me a little wave.

I keep replaying that whole scene in my head now, as I lie here staring into the dark, and it makes me feel all warm inside.

And then, just when I've managed to get rid of the nagging thought that something is still very wrong, it always comes crashing back in: Elspeth.

But the more I think about her, the more I wonder if she's gone. Maybe she went back to 1692 while Zachariah and I were gone.

But according to history, she never was seen again.

Then I sit straight up in bed, remembering something.

I never went back and checked the "History of Seacliffe" booklet Katie gave me. How could I forget? I have to see if anything has changed.

I remember that I last saw the blue paper booklet on the coffee table in the keeping room the other night. It's got to still be there.

I get out of bed and pull on my bathrobe, then tiptoe out into the dark hallway. It's well past midnight, and everyone is asleep. I can hear my father snoring loudly, and I remember hearing Great-Uncle William's snores from all the way down in the keeping room. It must run in the family.

I quietly slip downstairs. There's a full moon out, so it's pretty easy to make my way through the house without turning on any lights.

In the keeping room, I hurry over to the table and start searching through the piles of magazines and newspapers that have accumulated.

There it is.

My fingers have just touched the pamphlet when I hear a footstep directly behind me.

Before I can turn around, something cool and sharp is against my bare neck and a low voice says into my ear, "Make one sound, and I shall kill thee instantly."

TWENTY-TWO

"Where is he?" Elspeth asks, her fury barely controlled.

I remain motionless, still poised with my fingers against the program, too frightened to speak.

She moves her hand slightly, enough to press the blade of the cleaver more closely against my throat.

"Answer me!" she whispers harshly. "What hath thou done with him?"

"I . . . I haven't done anything, Elspeth. Please . . ."

She increases the pressure on the blade. "Where is he? I command thee to tell me now!"

"He's gone." I say in a strangled-sounding whisper.

"Gone?"

"1692," I say briefly, then realize I made a mistake. He's in 1691 . . .

"Why did he go back?"

"He . . ." I swallow hard, then tell her the truth. "He's trying to save Felicity."

"He must not interfere!" she bites out. "I must stop him . . ."

"You'd better hurry then," I say, closing my eyes and praying this will work. "There's no time to waste, Elspeth."

"Remain silent, or you shall die!" she says harshly, gripping my still-sore arm with bony fingers that dig painfully into my skin. But with her other hand, she's taking the blade away from my neck.

I exhale gratefully, then gulp when I feel it poking into my back.

"Walk," she orders me, yanking on my arm and turning me toward the secret cupboard.

She steers me over there, still holding the knife in my back.

Then she turns me around so that she can look at me, one arm still wrapped around me so that the blade is still digging into the layers of my robe and nightgown.

In the silvery light that spills in through the window, I can see the hard lines of her face and the glittering hatred in her inky eyes.

"Do not assume that thou will be safe if I leave. Make no mistake—I shall return," she warns me in a guttural voice. She moves the knife and I hear a quiet ripping sound as it tears at the fabric of my robe. "I shall make thee pay."

I just stare into her wicked eyes, numb with fear.

And then she carefully pulls the cleaver away and holds it up in front of me. Moonlight reflects off the sharp blade, and I fight the overwhelming impulse to back away.

She looks at the knife, then at me, and laughs. It's a low, evil sound.

"I shall return," she says again. With her other hand, she reaches into the folds of her skirt and produces a clump of dried leaves.

Her gaze is locked with mine as she backs inside the closet, still holding the blade up threateningly.

I'm fully aware that at any second, she can lunge forward and stab me with it.

I don't move.

I don't breathe.

I just stand, silent and motionless, watching as she pulls the inner door shut.

I hear her muffled voice start saying, "1692 . . . 1692 . . ."

And then there's only silence.

I let out a deep, shuddering breath, then hold still, listening.

Uh-oh.

I hear footsteps on the stairs.

"Abbey?"

It's my mother's voice.

I close the closet door and hurry into the hall. My mother is on the stairway, peering down at me over the railing.

"Abbey, what are you doing?" she asks suspiciously.

"I was thirsty . . . I just got a glass of water."

"Well, get back up into your room now," she tells me.

"Okay." I don't move.

She doesn't either. "Well?" she says expectantly.

"Can I just get something I left in the other room?"

"What is it?"

I hesitate, then say, "Nothing," and start up the stairs.

I'll wait until she's asleep again, then I'll sneak back down and get the book.

My mother goes into her room, and I hear my father stirring in bed and asking her something. She closes the door behind her, muffling her response.

In my room, I take off my robe and examine it. There, in the middle of the back, is a small, jagged tear. I shiver just looking at it, and her words echo in my head.

I shall return.

I don't doubt that she will. There's no way to stop her.

Trembling, I climb into my bed and prop the pillows against the iron backboard. Then I settle back to wait for the snoring to begin again.

* * *

I'm startled awake by a loud pounding sound.

My eyes snap open and I see that it's morning. My room is gray and gloomy, and rain is pattering against the roof.

But that wasn't what I heard.

I lie there, listening.

There it is again.

It's a terrible racket, and it's coming from the keeping room.

I jump out of bed, throw on shorts and a T-shirt, and go out into the hall. I can hear the rumble of masculine voices now, coming from downstairs, and more pounding.

I hurry down the stairs and stop short when I see what's below. The front hall is filled with furniture. It only takes me a few seconds to realize where it came from.

Puzzled, I move forward, weaving a path among the clutter of tables and chairs to the doorway to the keeping room.

I peer inside, then gasp.

My father, Joe, and Clarence are there, beside the fireplace, holding crowbars and hammers.

There's a big pile of splintered wood on the floor . . . and a gaping hole where the closet used to be.

"What are you doing?" I cry out, rushing forward.

"Abbey, stay out of here in your bare feet," my father says, turning around and catching sight of me. "You'll step on a nail or get a sliver or something."

I stop, still gaping. "But Dad, what's going on?"

"It's raining out, so we're working in here today. We're ripping out this closet so we can expand the doorway to the kitchen," he tells me, like I should know.

I just stare.

"Come on, Abbey, you knew that. Your mother and I told you all about the remodeling, remember?"

"I guess . . . I guess I wasn't paying attention," I say slowly.

"I guess not." He shakes his head, then turns back to Joe and says, "So you don't think it was unusual?"

"Nah—a lot of these old houses have hidden rooms and closets, Frank. Now let's get busy on this other side, here . . ."

Wide-eyed, I stand there, staring at the hole next to the fireplace. It's dawning on me now why Katie and I couldn't travel to the future yesterday . . .

"Abbey? What's the matter?"

. . . The closet was gone! And if we couldn't go forward, that means that Elspeth won't be able to either.

I heave an enormous sigh of relief, then realize that my father's talking to me.

"What, Dad?"

He looks exasperated. "I just asked you what's the matter."

"Nothing," I say hastily, backing out of the room. "Never mind."

In the hallway, I turn around and nearly trip over the coffee table. I glance down and see the "History of Seacliffe" pamphlet lying there.

Finally!

Eagerly, I reach down and grab it, then take the stairs to my room two at a time.

I close the door behind me, then flop down on my unmade bed and open the pamphlet.

Taking a deep breath, I flip through the first few pages, then stop at the one with the heading, "Witchcraft in Seacliffe."

In 1692, a reign of terror was spreading throughout New England, particularly through the small rural towns in the vicinity of Salem, Massachusetts . . .

I scan the paragraph that describes the Salem witch hunts, and pick up again at the next paragraph that begins,

Sadly, the quiet town of Seacliffe was not spared. On June 23, 1692, a young local girl was accused of witchcraft.

I take a deep breath and turn the page.

The first thing that jumps out at me is the name *Elspeth Andrewes.*

I close my eyes, overtaken by a sinking feeling.

Can it be that nothing has changed—that Elspeth accused Felicity and she was executed after all?

I force myself to open my eyes and keep reading.

Elspeth Andrewes, a teenage servant girl, mysteriously appeared in the home of Josiah Crane in the middle of the night. The frightened Crane family claimed she had suddenly materialized in a first floor closet out of thin air, and she was arrested under suspicion of witchcraft. She was brought to trial shortly afterward, found guilty, and sentenced to death. Elspeth Andrewes was hung on Seacliffe's commons on July 1, 1693, the only witch ever to be tried and executed in Seacliffe.

I close the booklet, shaking my head. I know the witch trials were a tragedy, but I can't help feeling a twinge of satisfaction that Elspeth Andrewes got a taste of her own medicine.

I sit there, contemplating what I just read.

Then I look at the booklet again.

I can't help wondering whatever happened to Felicity and Zachariah. Maybe there's a clue in there.

I flip quickly through the pages again, then pause and backtrack . . .

A name caught my eye on one of the pages.

Here, under the heading, "Seacliffe the Site of Revolutionary War Battle."

In 1775, John Turner, a Massachusetts minuteman, was the first soldier killed in the battle with the British at Lexington and Concord. He was the son of Abigail Wellbourne Turner of Boston. John Turner was given a hero's burial in the Wellbourne family plot in Seacliffe's North Burial Ground, where he lies beside his grandparents Zachariah and Felicity Crane Wellbourne, two of Seacliffe's most respected citizens.

Zachariah and Felicity Crane Wellbourne.

They were married, and they had a daughter—a daughter named Abigail.

I remember my final conversation with Zachariah.

"I'm going to miss you," I'd told him as he stood poised in the doorway of the secret cupboard.

And he'd responded, *"I shall never forget thee, Abigail. Some day, I vow, I will find a way to thank thee."*

Abigail Wellbourne Turner.

I smile and whisper, "You're welcome, Zachariah."

EPILOGUE

July 4, 1976

The old North Burial ground on the edge of town is deserted today. Everyone in Seacliffe has been lined up along Main Street since dawn for what the chamber of commerce is billing the second biggest Bicentennial parade in New England. The biggest is in Bristol, Rhode Island, a town my husband and I drove through on our way to Newport for a second honeymoon last year.

We've been married for ten years this summer. Everyone said it wouldn't work out—that we were too young. I was only nineteen and he was twenty-one, and we had a one-month engagement. We were married in a sunset ceremony on the beach the day after he graduated from Boston University. Since he doesn't have any brothers, Peter and Paul were co-best-men. They looked so grown up in their suits. Katie was the maid of honor, in the pale pink eyelet dress she'd picked out, even though I'd wanted her to wear olive green chiffon.

Josie, my only bridesmaid, wore the olive green. She whispered into my ear, right before we left on our honeymoon, that people were saying I was pregnant. She knew the truth—that we were afraid he'd be drafted and sent to Vietnam.

It happened anyway, a year after our wedding. By then, I

really *was* pregnant. But he turned out to be 4-F, thanks to an old football knee injury. And he was there, pacing the waiting room, that Christmas morning when our first child was born.

Felicity.

The name seemed only fitting when I saw the reddish tint in our baby's newborn fuzz and looked into her bright blue eyes. They're brown now, like mine, and her hair's a sandy color like her daddy's, but every so often, when the sun hits it just right, I see fiery highlights, and I remember.

I walk up over a little rise, and I see it there, ahead. The Wellbourne family plot.

I hear cannons going off in the distance on the commons, signaling that the parade is about to start. The kids will be anxious—I have to hurry.

Stopping in front of the two oldest, crumbling stones, I stoop down to pull a few weeds. Then I close my eyes, say a little prayer, and lay the flowers—red and white roses tied with a bright blue satin ribbon—between the graves.

Only minutes ago, I laid a similar bouquet at another spot down the hill, that one a soldier's grave, only four years old and marked with an American flag.

Now I scan these worn markers as I've done dozens of times over the years, and as always, a lump chokes my throat.

Here lies Zachariah Wellbourne, beloved husband of Felicity; b. March 17, 1675; called home January 10, 1763.

Here lies Felicity Wellbourne, beloved wife of Zachariah; b. September 1, 1676; called home April 25, 1763.

She'd only lived a few months without him. I read in an old book in the Seacliffe library that her daughter Abigail always said Felicity had died of a broken heart. Maybe it's true. And now, somewhere, she and her beloved Zachariah are together again.

I sigh and look up at the clear blue summer sky.

"Mommy!"

Turning, I see little Petey running toward me. His four-year-old legs are short and still dimply with baby fat.

"Come on, Mommy, Daddy says to hurry up or we'll miss seeing Uncle Paul leading the parade in his police car."

"All right, sweetie." I take his small hand and squeeze it.

He looks back over his shoulder as we walk back down the rise. "Who's buried there, Mommy?"

"Old friends of mine," I tell him.

"Did they die in the war like Uncle Peter did?"

I swallow hard and shake my head. "No. They died a long, long time ago."

"Were they heroes like Uncle Peter was?"

I smile. "In a way." I've told Petey and Felicity all about their brave uncle, who saved the lives of dozens of men in the faraway jungle before being killed in a surprise attack four years ago—a month before my son was born.

We pass his grave again on the way to the old iron gates of the cemetery. There are the bright red geraniums my parents planted on Memorial Day, and the wreath Paul and his fiancée put there this morning.

Just beyond the gates, I spot my eight-year-old daughter, who's starting to look so like her Aunt Katie. She's sitting cross-legged on the grass, her nose stuck in a Nancy Drew book. My tall, handsome husband is leaning on the wood-paneled station wagon, making a big show of tapping his foot impatiently and glancing at the watch on his sun-bronzed forearm.

"Come on, New Yo-awk," he calls, waving. "Get a move on."

Petey runs ahead. When I reach the car, I throw my arms around Riley and give him a squeeze.

"What's that for?" he asks as the kids scramble into the backseat of the station wagon.

"I just felt like it."

He shakes his head, grinning. "Get into the car, Mrs. Kennedy."

I do, and we head back down Route 1A, past the sign that reads, WELCOME TO PATRIOTIC SEACLIFFE, AMERICA'S HOME-TOWN.

About the Author

Wendy Corsi Staub lives with her husband, Mark, in Bristol, Rhode Island. She is the author of SUMMER LIGHTNING, which won the Romance Writers of America's RITA award for best young adult romance, and HALLOWEEN PARTY, a young adult horror novel. Wendy loves hearing from her readers and you may write to her c/o Pinnacle Books. Please include a self-addressed stamped envelope if you wish a response.

Please turn the page for
an exciting sneak preview of
Wendy Corsi Staub's
OBSESSION

ONE

Megan McKenna glanced at her chunky gold bracelet watch as she followed her boyfriend up the walk toward Zoe's house. "We're pretty late," she told Shea, reaching up to smooth her long, dark brown hair. "Zoe will probably be annoyed."

"Zoe's *always* annoyed. She'll get over it." He reached back and caught her hand, giving her fingers a squeeze.

And even though they'd been going out for over six months, since February break, she still felt all fluttery at the warm skin-to-skin contact.

Maybe eventually, she'd stop feeling this way whenever Shea touched her. Maybe holding hands with him would become no big deal.

Maybe.

But for now, it was still a semi-big deal.

And so was what had just happened in his car.

He had picked her up on time for the party. But instead of heading directly over toward Zoe's, he'd turned onto Soundview Drive. The winding, tree-lined road led to the quiet park where Meg and Shea had spent a lot of time this summer—after dark, when the picnicking families and church groups, kite-fliers and frisbee-players had all gone home.

There, parked in their usual isolated spot in a grove of

pine trees, they had spent some feverish stolen moments. It was Shea who put on the brakes, as always, pulling back, straightening his clothes, and saying, "We better stop while we still can."

And as always, Meg had thought, *While* you *still can.*

He'd started the car and driven toward Zoe's while Meg checked her flushed face in the visor mirror and reapplied her lipstick with a trembling hand . . . and wondered how Shea could always stop them from going too far when she felt powerless to.

When she *wanted* to go further.

But . . . wasn't it supposed to be the other way around?

Wasn't the girl supposed to protect her virtue?

If it was up to Meg, her virtue would have been history by now. She'd known, from the first time she'd been alone with Shea last winter, that she was ready to stop the flirting, teasing games she'd been playing with all the guys she'd gone out with until now. She'd known Shea was *the one*—that this thing with him could be serious; that she'd wanted it to be—*expected* it to be.

None of her friends at the Adamson-Swift School—the friends who had long ago dubbed her Sister Meg—would suspect that Shea Alcott was a virgin, too.

Not that Meg was a hundred percent positive about that. He'd never *told* her he was a virgin, and he'd never asked about her status. They didn't talk about that stuff. They just parked and went at it until Shea stopped just before the point of no return, and Meg invariably felt frustrated—and guilty for not being the one to pull back first. Not that she ever protested or tried to push things further. That wasn't her style.

Now, they climbed the wide steps in front of the sprawling brick colonial where Zoe Cunningham's end-of-the-summer bash was in full swing. Shea let go of Meg's hand before reaching out to knock on the massive wooden door.

And Meg sighed inwardly and wished he didn't have a *thing* about being affectionate in front of other people. She wouldn't have minded making an entrance holding hands—especially since Shea's old girlfriend, Maura Nealey, was supposed to be here.

"Don't bother knocking," Meg said, reaching out and turning the doorknob. "They'll all be outside in the back. No one will hear."

The door was unlocked, as she'd known it would be. She pushed it open and walked into the familiar center hall, with its sweeping, broad staircase and hand-painted tile floor.

"Come on," Meg said to Shea, leading the way through the living room, dining room, and sunny glassed-in porch that Tara Cunningham called "the conservatory."

From there, they could see the crowd on the three levels of wooden decks that descended gradually to the lush, landscaped yard—Mrs. Cunningham called it "the garden"—with its spotlights, statues, benches, and winding flagstone paths.

Meg and Shea slipped out through the double French doors and were immediately engulfed by the crowd.

"It's about time," Zoe said, grabbing Meg's arm and tossing her smooth, pale hair. "Where *were* you guys?"

"Sorry," Meg said, glancing at Shea, who was being pulled away by a chattering Allison Maine, an irritating little blonde with a penchant for flirting with other people's boyfriends.

He gave Meg a helpless, *sorry, what can I do?* shrug.

"Meggie!" a high-pitched voice squealed in her ear, and she found herself wrapped in a viselike embrace and the strong scent of expensive perfume that was her friend Chasey Norman's trademark.

"You're back!" Chasey had spent the summer in the south of France with her mother and her mother's new boyfriend. "I thought you weren't coming home until Labor Day."

Chasey shrugged and shook her head, her riot of silky red curls bobbing furiously. "I didn't want to hang out there for another whole week. I mean, I was really getting homesick."

"For Crawford Corners?"

"Yeah, right, Meg. The town beach really compares to the French Riviera." Chasey shook her head. "I was actually homesick for you guys." She draped her sun-bronzed arms around Meg's and Zoe's shoulders. "I can't wait to, like, fill you in about everything."

"I can't wait to hear about it, Chase," Zoe said distractedly, "but right now I have to go rescue my cousin from Andy Dorner."

"Andy Dorner? *Eeuuh.*" Chasey made a face.

"Your cousin's here?" Meg asked Zoe. "I thought she wasn't coming until your parents get back from California."

"Yeah, well, that's what I thought, too. But she drove up from Louisiana with some kid who needed to get here by this weekend. I didn't find out she'd be here early till she called me two days ago. What could I say? That she had to stay in a hotel until my parents got back? But she's actually pretty cool, and she swore not to tell my mother about this party."

" 'Mirabelle the Southern Belle' turned out to be *cool?* You're kidding." Meg had been listening to Zoe complain all summer about how her cousin from Louisiana was going to be coming in the fall to attend the private college in nearby Spring City, and how Zoe was going to be stuck entertaining her.

"She's cool enough not to deserve being slimed by Andy Dorner," Zoe said, and hurried away.

Meg turned to Chasey. "So, Chase, tell me about France. Did you hook up with that guy—what was his name? Jean?"

"Jacques. I hooked up with him for about two seconds before I realized he was a real jerk. He really changed since last year."

"Maybe he was just on his best behavior because he was an exchange student over here."

Chasey shrugged. "Whatever. I blew him off pretty fast."

"So what else is new," Meg said, shaking her head. Chasey blew *everyone* off.

"No, listen, Meg, I met this guy from New York when I was flying back yesterday—his name's Billy, and he's, like, gorgeous."

"Oh, yeah?" Meg felt something furry brush her bare legs and looked down to see Mrs. Cunningham's Persian cat, Jewel. Meg sensed that she wanted to be picked up. Not wanting to get fur all over the black brocade top she was wearing, Meg crouched down and petted the purring animal. "Good kitty. Good girl."

"He's gonna be a sophomore at NYU, and he's driving up to see me next weekend," Chasey was saying.

"Who?" Meg asked, glancing up.

"Billy! Who was I just talking about? Meg, what's up with you and that stupid cat? She always gravitates right to you. Whenever I go near her, she hisses at me."

"Well, no one likes to be called stupid, Chase. And you know Jewel—Zoe said she hisses at everyone."

"Except you."

As if to punctuate Chasey's remark, Jewel rested her front paws lovingly on the tops of Meg's thighs and gave a pleased, *"meow."*

Chasey shook her head. "It's so weird how animals are

always trying to climb all over you. What are you, like, Dr. Doolittle?"

Meg rolled her eyes and was about to reply when Zoe reappeared with a willowy stranger in tow.

"Guys, this is Mirabelle Moreau," she said. "'Mir', these are my two best friends, Meg McKenna and Chasey Norman."

Meg gently moved Jewel's paws from her legs and stood up.

The girl wasn't the Miss America contestant clone Meg had expected of someone Zoe had dubbed "Mirabelle the Southern Belle." Instead of a blond bouffant, she had long, silky brown hair that hung loose to the middle of her back, parted in the middle and tucked casually behind her ears. Rather than fair, delicate skin, she had a healthy glow, and she wasn't wearing any makeup. Her clothes were simple, too—cutoff Levi's jeans and a plain off-white T-shirt.

"Nice to meet y'all," Mirabelle drawled. She said nice, *"nahs."*

Chasey said, "Wow, where are you from? You have this amazing accent."

"Ahm from *Nu-awlins,"* was the reply.

Chasey blinked.

"She's from New Orleans," Zoe translated briefly, then said, "Mirabelle, you can hang with these guys while I go inside and make sure no one's in my parents' bedroom. I saw Deb and Joel heading in a few minutes ago, and ol' Tara will freak if she finds anything out of place when she gets home Tuesday."

Zoe dashed toward the house without a backward glance.

Meg turned to Mirabelle and was startled to find that the girl's strange, light green eyes were narrowed intently on her, as though she were pondering something. She cleared her throat and shifted uncomfortably. "So, Mirabelle, have you ever been in Crawford Corners before?"

"I was here last spring with my mother to visit the college. We stayed here with Aunt Tara and Uncle Greg, but Zoe wasn't around. I haven't seen her since her family came down for Mardi Gras about four years ago."

Chasey shot Meg a blank look that meant, *What* the heck did she say?

It took a second for Meg to decipher Mirabelle's drawled reply. "Oh, that's right, you were here around Easter time, right? That was when Zoe came with me and my family to Florida for a week."

"Yes." Mirabelle was still watching her.

Meg wished she would stop. The rapt expression in her pale eyes was disconcerting. Meg caught her bottom lip in her top teeth. *Why's she looking at me this way?*

At her feet, Jewel purred and rubbed against her bare leg. Meg reached down and stroked her fur again, then looked up to see that Mirabelle was still fixated on her.

"Have you ever been to France, Mirabelle?" Chasey asked brightly, swaying slightly back and forth in time to the music that was blasting from the stereo speakers.

"France?" The girl shifted her gaze briefly from Meg. "No, I never have been."

"Really? You should go sometime. I just spent the summer on the Riviera, and it was great."

"How nice," Mirabelle said politely, and shrugged. "I've never been abroad."

Meg noticed that Jewel was now rubbing affectionately against Mirabelle's ankles.

"You *haven't?*" Chasey sounded surprised. *"Never?"*

Oh, come off it, Chase, Meg thought. She hated when her friend slipped into this act. There were few among their crowd at Adamson-Swift who hadn't been to Europe, and Chasey liked to think she was more worldly and well-traveled than most.

Meg knew her friend was basically bighearted and could usually forgive her for her snobbish tendencies. Chasey had grown up in a lower-middle-class neighborhood in Stamford, moving to Crawford Corners only about eight years ago when her mother—a buxom, predatory gold digger—divorced her father and married a rich older businessman with a severe heart condition. He had died a few summers back, and though Chasey and her mother still lived among the elite, they were less tolerated now that their blue-blooded benefactor was out of the picture. Meg knew Chasey was forever trying to convince herself—and others—that she belonged here.

Now she gave Mirabelle a wide-eyed stare and said, "Why haven't you ever been to Europe?"

Mirabelle shrugged. "I don't like to fly," she said, and stooped down to give the cat a brief pat on the head.

"You're *kidding!*" Chasey said. "Why not?"

"Because I was warned not to," Mirabelle said simply, rising, flicking her steady gaze back to Meg.

"Huh?" Chasey said.

An odd feeling stole over Meg. She couldn't seem to tear her eyes away from Mirabelle's. "What do you mean, you were warned not to?"

Mirabelle glanced briefly at Chasey, then turned back to Meg and shrugged. "It's a long story."

Meg frowned and was about to pursue it when Shea suddenly appeared beside her.

"Hey, I'm back."

"It's about time," Meg said. She stepped closer to him and fought the urge to slip her hand casually into his, knowing he wouldn't like it. "Shea, this is Zoe's cousin, Mirabelle . . ."

"Moreau," the girl supplied.

"That's right, Moreau. She just moved up here from New Orleans to go to college. Mirabelle, this is my boyfriend, Shea Alcott."

"Nice to meet you," Shea said smoothly, and shook her hand. "Where are you going to school?"

"Wainwright College."

Shea nodded. "Are you living on campus?"

"Yes, but I can't get into the dorms until Wednesday, so I'm staying here at the Cunninghams' for a few days."

"Geez, Shea," Chasey cut in. "You haven't seen *me* since June—aren't you going to say welcome back or anything?"

He grinned. "Welcome back, Chasey—how's it going? When'd you get home?"

"It's going great," she said, looking relieved to have the focus move away from Mirabelle, "and I just flew into JFK last night." Chasey shot a pointed look in Zoe's cousin's direction.

Again, Meg wondered what Mirabelle had meant by being warned not to fly.

And again, she felt uncomfortable when she noticed that those light green eyes were still fixed on her, probing, as though Mirabelle could see straight inside to Meg's very soul.

As the plane rattled and thumped its way to a lower altitude, Candra Bowen decided she hated flying.

Not that she'd ever done it before.

And not that she was afraid of crashing, or anything like that.

She *knew,* with a familiar certainty that should have calmed her, that they weren't going to crash.

So she wasn't *afraid.*

Just . . . uneasy. Because up here, hurtling through the air thousands of feet above the ground, she had no control over anything that happened.

And Candra liked to be in control.

She glanced out the window, hoping to see something, but there was only the same milky mist that had been there ever since they'd reached the mainland.

It had been several hours now since Candra had stared through the window and bid a silent farewell as Jamaica's mountainous countryside gave way to the sparkling aqua waters of the Caribbean Sea. For the first time in all her seventeen years, she had left the island that had always been home.

She'd been ready—hell, she'd been *longing* for this day ever since Grandmother had told her their employers, the Drayers, were moving back to the States and wanted to take them along. But as eager as she'd been to leave Jamaica behind, Candra had been shocked to feel a tear trickling down her smooth brown cheek as the plane ascended and the tiny land mass had vanished for good.

Candra had quickly wiped the tear away and glanced at Grandmother to see if she, too, was emotional. But the old woman's eyes had been squeezed tightly shut, and she was wincing and gripping the armrests as though bracing for an inevitable collision. She had pretty much stayed that way for the past few hours.

Grandmother had never flown before, either.

Now, as the FASTEN SEAT BELTS sign suddenly *ding*ed and lit up again, Candra heard her grandmother give a little gasp.

"Don't worry," Candra said, turning toward her. "We'll be fine."

Rosamund Bowen looked terrified. Her dark chocolate-colored skin seemed tinged with a chalky hue. "How do you know?" she asked her granddaughter.

How do you think I know? Candra wanted to ask her. *How do I know anything? You're the one who taught me to listen to the voices in my mind. And right now, they're telling me we're going to be fine.*

But she didn't say that. The woman sitting in the aisle seat on the other side of her grandmother had her nose buried in a paperback, but she looked like the nosy type who might be eavesdropping.

She'd glanced up sharply earlier when she'd heard Candra call Rosamund "Grandmother." Candra had known what she was thinking. *That black woman is her grandmother?*

Candra's skin was so pale that people always assumed she was white. Actually, her mother had been, but her father, Rosamund's son, had been black.

"Didn't you hear the pilot a few minutes ago?" Candra asked her worried grandmother. "He said it's almost time to land in New York City. We're coming down—that's why it's so bumpy."

The plane lurched again. Her grandmother gave a little shriek and clutched Candra's wrist.

Candra rolled her eyes and said again, "Don't worry."

Then she turned back toward the window to see what she could see.

Nothing—just a thick cloud bank.

When would she be able to catch a glimpse of New York City? Mrs. Drayer had told her that she might be able to see the Statue of Liberty before they landed.

Imagine that—the Statue of Liberty.

Did the Drayers have a better view from where they were sitting now, up in first class?

No, Candra told herself. *Of course they don't. They can't see any more than you can.*

Still, she wondered what it was like up there, beyond the curtain that was kept carefully drawn to keep the rest of the passengers from peering into that privileged cabin.

Candra knew she should be grateful to her grandmother's employer for buying her and Rosamund their plane tickets, and she hadn't really expected to be in first class. But that didn't stop her from resenting the Drayers, who, of course, were.

What were they doing up there, right now? Candra closed her eyes and conjured a mental picture of the four of them.

Craig, who at seventeen was exactly Candra's age, would be playing with one of his hand-held computer games and saying, "Yes!" every time he scored a point. His mother would shush him, and he would naturally ignore her. He was good-looking in a lazy, cocky way, and acted as though he had the run of the world. He never lost an opportunity to remind Candra that she was "the help."

His sister Jane was no less self-centered and snobby, but at least she was quieter about it. At fifteen, she was just starting to lose the baby fat that had plagued her, and showed every hint of becoming a lean, Waspy matron like her mother. Right now, Jane would be wearing her CD Walkman and bobbing her head in time to the music.

Monica, Candra knew, was probably flipping idly through her copy of *Vogue* and checking her Rolex every few seconds. She was the perfect, punctual type and would know exactly what time they were supposed to land. In a few minutes, she would take out her jewel-encrusted compact and powder her straight, small nose before carefully gliding a silver tube of burgundy lipstick over her thin lips.

Jonas, her husband, would be beside her, sipping a cocktail—not his first. His perpetually ruddy complexion attested to the fact that he was a drinker. He would undoubtedly be leafing through a ubiquitous sheaf of business papers on his lap.

Jonas Drayer was a powerful, important real estate developer, and Candra knew that he was largely responsible for the exclusive new Coral Sands resort that had opened last month in Ocho Rios. Before that, he had been involved with the sparkling new Sea Breeze resort, which was now invariably filled to capacity.

The Drayers were unlike other American corporate families who relocated to Jamaica, then hightailed it back to "civilization" as soon as their business was finished. They had been on the island since the tourist industry had revived in the late seventies. Jonas worked for a large real estate development company based in southwestern Connecticut, and he and his colleagues had played a major role in turning Ocho Rios into a resort town.

The Drayers had lived in the hills above the port, where several celebrities owned estates. Their home was lavish, with two swimming pools, a tennis court, landscaped gardens, and sweeping views of the sea. Candra and her grandmother, who was their housekeeper, had lived in the servants' quarters that were built into the sloping land at the back of the big house, underneath the main floor.

When Candra was little, Craig and Jane had been her playmates, and she had liked them, though they were spoiled and liked to brag about the new toys they were always getting. But as the Drayer children grew older and were sent to boarding schools in the States, the bond between them and Candra had been replaced by an invisible line that she knew better than to try to cross. These days, neither Craig nor Jane tried to hide the fact that they looked down on her from their lofty perches, and it had been a decade since Candra had had a real conversation with either of them.

In the years while her children were growing up, Monica had spent a lot of time back home in Connecticut. Lately when she had been in Jamaica, she had talked incessantly about "home," and so had Craig and Jane. Candra knew that the three of them had finally pressured Jonas into this move back to the States.

She knew, too, that it had been Jonas's idea to take Rosamund and Candra with them. Unlike his wife and children, he had considered them part of the family—at least, to the extent that he was concerned about what might happen to them after the Drayers left Jamaica.

Rosamund had been working for the family since before Candra was born. Good jobs were hard to come by, and Jonas had told Candra's grandmother that he hated to think of the two of them living in some shantytown like many of the locals did. So he had offered to move them to Connecticut, and Rosamund had accepted. Candra knew her grandmother probably would never have agreed to leave Jamaica if her sister Letitia hadn't happened to be a maid on an estate in Greenwich, Connecticut. According to Jonas, that was only about twenty minutes away from his house in Crawford Corners. And Spring City, where Aunt Tish lived, was even closer.

Candra, too, had been excited about the prospect of moving to America. There, she knew, she would finally have the opportunity to make something of herself. And someday, she kept telling herself fiercely, *she* would be flying in first class.

There was another *ding* and the pilot's voice came over

the intercom. "Ladies and Gentlemen, please fasten your seatbelts, put your tray tables up, and bring your seats to an upright position as we begin our final approach into John F. Kennedy airport. We should have you on the ground in six minutes."

This is it, Candra thought, catching her bottom lip in her top teeth in anticipation. After all that waiting, she was finally about to land in this new country and begin her new life.

The clouds were beginning to thin, and she focused intently on the window, wondering if she'd get to see the Statue of Liberty in the harbor after all.

But as the clouds became mere wisps and the view opened up, she saw that they were over land, and flying low. Fascinated, Candra studied the tops of houses and buildings and trees, and noted the miniature cars moving about the gridlike streets.

Then she heard it.

The voice.

As always, it was a mere whisper, slipping subtly into her mind so that she was barely aware of it at first. She narrowed her black eyes and strained to hear what it was telling her.

She's down there . . . You have to find her . . .

Candra frowned, puzzled.

Who? she asked herself. *Who's down there?*

But there was no answer.

Only an echo that said simply, and urgently, *Find her.*

"Hi, Meg," said a voice behind her.

Startled, Meg jumped and spun around to see Mirabelle sitting on the window seat. Jewel was in her lap, looking contented as Zoe's cousin stroked her.

"I'm sorry," the girl drawled. "I didn't mean to scare you."

"It's okay." Meg pressed a fist against her wildly pounding heart and shook her head.

She had just come out of Zoe's bathroom, where she had been trying to remove as much cat fur as possible from her black shirt. Jewel had insisted on jumping into her lap while she'd been sitting on a bench out on the deck, and she had found herself covered in fine white hair. Finally, Zoe had come along, chased the cat away, and told Meg where to find a lint brush.

Mirabelle hadn't been here in Zoe's bedroom when Meg had passed through it a few minutes ago.

Did she follow me up here? Meg wondered, then discarded the idea. *Don't be ridiculous. Why would she do that?*

Maybe because she's been staring at you all night.

Meg shifted her weight and said, "Well, I guess I'll get back to the party." She started to move away, knowing somehow that Mirabelle was going to stop her.

She was right.

"Wait, Meg, don't go," the girl said, standing up and setting the cat lightly on the floor. Jewel promptly stretched and trotted over to rub against Meg's ankles again.

"I came up here because I wanted to talk to you about something," Mirabelle said.

So she was following me.

"You did?" Meg asked, trying not to appear as thrown as she felt. "What is it?"

"Before, when I said that thing about not flying?"

She nodded.

"Well," Mirabelle continued, "I thought I should explain what I meant. I didn't want to say anything in front of your friend, but I knew you would understand."

"What do you mean?"

Mirabelle moved closer to where she was standing, and idly picked up a crystal figurine from Zoe's dresser. "I mean," she said, running her fingertips over the piece, "that there are certain things you just don't tell certain people. But the second I saw you, I sensed that you were someone who . . ." She trailed off and looked up at Meg. "I knew that you were like me."

"Like you?"

"Meg, I've been getting vibes from you the second I got here."

Meg fought the urge to take a step backward. Suddenly it crossed her mind that Zoe's cousin might be a lesbian.

Is she putting the moves on me? she wondered. In a way, that would almost be a relief. At least, it would make sense.

"The reason I don't *fly,*" Mirabelle said abruptly, "is that I was warned not to."

Meg blinked. "Excuse me?"

"I was warned by a witch."

"A . . . *witch?*"

"Uh-huh. Cecile's my neighbors' housekeeper back home. She practices voodoo, and she taught me."

Meg just stared.

"Anyway, she's psychic—most witches are—and she told me that I should stay away from airplanes because she saw a lot of negative energy in me about that. That was years ago. I haven't flown since." Mirabelle carefully set down the crystal figurine, folded her arms, and looked directly at Meg. "Now I don't need Cecile to tell me things. I'm in tune with my own sixth sense."

She's crazy—she must be. Just act like you understand what she's talking about.

"Cecile taught me how some people are born with . . . certain powers," Mirabelle went on. *"She* was. And I was, too. My father comes from an old Creole family. He doesn't know it, but his grandmother was a voodoo priestess. Cecile told me that. She said I must have gotten my abilities from her. Cecile taught me how to cultivate them, and how to recognize the same sensitivity in other people. I hardly ever meet anyone who has it, but I sensed it in you right away."

"In me?" Meg echoed.

Mirabelle peered closely at her for a long moment. "Maybe you weren't even aware of it. Meg, I'm sorry. I thought you might be . . ."

"Be what?"

"Practicing."

"Practicing *what?*"

"Witchcraft."

Now Meg did take a step backward. She couldn't seem to find her voice.

"I'm really sorry," Mirabelle said again. "You look really freaked out. I didn't mean to scare you or anything. It's no big deal."

No big deal?

"It's okay." Meg's voice came out slightly hoarse.

"I guess I could be wrong, but—" Mirabelle shook her head. "Look, Meg, forget about it, okay?"

"Okay." She hesitated. "I'd better get back downstairs."

"Right. Do me a favor?"

"Yes?" Oh, God. What was Mirabelle going to ask of her?

"Can you just tell Zoe I went to bed? I don't mean to be antisocial, but I'm still zonked after that long drive."

"Sure," Meg said, almost sighing with relief.

"Great." The girl yawned and stretched, then kicked off her sandals and bent to pick them up.

In that moment, Mirabelle seemed just like anyone else. Not like a witch.

Don't be ridiculous, Meg. She's not a witch!

But she said she was.

"G'night," Meg said swiftly to Mirabelle, and left Zoe's room without a backward glance.

As she hurried down the stairs, she let the rest of the thought enter her mind.

And she said you were a witch, too.

Candra had never been in a stretch limousine before.

This one was shiny black, and it had been waiting for the Drayers right outside the chaotic airport terminal.

At first, Candra hadn't expected to ride in the limo, and she didn't think Rosamund did, either. But after Craig, Jane, and Monica had clambered in, the chauffeur stood holding the door expectantly, and Jonas had given Candra's arm a little nudge.

"Go ahead," he'd said. "Get in."

She'd looked at him in surprise, then ducked into the plush, dim interior, thinking, *this is going to be the first time of many.*

Now that she was here in America, she would waste no time figuring out how to become as wealthy—no, wealthier—than the Drayers. And someday, she would treat Craig and Jane with as much contempt as they directed toward her.

I'll show them.

It was a familiar refrain, one that had been running through her head since childhood.

She settled on the seat facing the three Drayers, with Jonas on one side of her and Rosamund—still looking numb from the flight—on the other.

The car seemed to glide along the highways, and Candra spent the whole trip sneaking furtive glances out the tinted windows. It felt strange to be driving on the right-hand side of the road, with oncoming traffic way off to the left. She marveled at how every road was wide and paved. Here, there was no livestock wandering in the streets, and the houses she saw beyond the highway were all set close to each other, in neat rows.

She didn't want Craig and Jane to catch her looking excited or intrigued. They were both doing their best to act blasé about the whole trip, but Candra could tell that even they were excited about being back in New York.

"Over there, Candra," Monica said at one point, "is Manhattan."

She glanced out the window and saw the glittering skyline to their left. Only a narrow band of river separated them from it.

"Oh, geez, we're not going through the city, are we?" Craig asked. "That'll take forever."

We're not? Candra thought, disappointed.

"No, we're taking the Triborough," Jonas told him.

Candra was riding backward, so she could watch the skyline fall away behind them without anyone noticing that she was staring at it.

Someday, she thought, *I'm going to be a part of that. I'm going to buy things in the most expensive stores and eat in the finest restaurants . . .*

Candra lost herself in her familiar fantasies.

Soon they were zooming over an enormous bridge, and shortly afterward, the road opened up and there wasn't as much to look at. They seemed to be out of the city, and though the road was still lined with buildings and houses and neon signs, everything was more spread out now.

"Look, Daddy," Jane said, reaching across and tapping her father's knee. "See that sign?"

"Welcome to Connecticut," Jonas read. "We're almost home, honey."

Almost home. Candra's first limousine ride was almost over.

As the big car sped through the dark night, that same feeling she'd had on the plane started to come over her again.

The feeling that she was getting closer than ever to something—or someone—significant.

She listened intently for the voices in her mind again, but they weren't speaking to her now. This was more of a vague sensation that she was connected to this place somehow. She needed to find that connection, whatever it was.

The feeling grew stronger as the limousine finally slowed and left the highway.

"The town of Crawford Corners is about a mile down the road that way," Jonas told Candra and Rosamund, pointing in the opposite direction from the one in which they were turning. "We live over here, by the water."

Rosamund gave a polite nod.

Candra stared absently out the window, focused intently on her intuition.

Her instincts were telling her that whatever she was supposed to find here in America was nearby, waiting for her.